"The *Enterprise* herself could blow up within thirty seconds of engaging warp drive."

"What's the risk of a core breakdown?" asked Captain April.

Chief Engineer Powell shook his head. "I'd say roughly seventy percent."

"Seventy-one point three eight seven percent," Spock corrected. "That is a closer approximation."

April turned and glared at him. "What's this civilian doing on my bridge?"

"I will leave if you wish," Spock said. "However, I believe I may be of use. I have some experience with computer languages, and I may be able to repair your problem."

"Sir," Pike said, "nine minutes left. Mr. Spock is an extremely gifted young man. It couldn't hurt to let him have a try."

April nodded. "Very well. Take the science officer's console, Mr. Spock."

Available from MINSTREL Books

STAR TREK®
STARFLEET ACADEMY®

#1: CRISIS ON VULCAN

BRAD AND BARBARA STRICKLAND

Interior illustrations by
Todd Cameron Hamilton

A
MINSTREL®
BOOK

Published by POCKET BOOKS
New York   London   Toronto   Sydney   Tokyo   Singapore

A MINSTREL PAPERBACK *Original*

A Minstrel Book published by
POCKET BOOKS, a division of Simon & Schuster Inc.
1230 Avenue of the Americas, New York, NY 10020

ISBN: 0-671-00078-0

First Minstrel Books printing August 1996

10 9 8 7 6 5 4 3 2 1

Cover art by Michael Herring

Printed in the U.S.A.

To Val and Ron Lindahn,

*Accomplished Artists, Fellow Trekkers,
and Treasured Friends*

STARFLEET TIMELINE

1969 Neil Armstrong walks on Earth's moon.

2156 Romulan Wars begin between Earth forces and the Romulan Star Empire.

2160 Romulan peace treaty signed, establishing the Neutral Zone.

2161 United Federation of Planets formed; Starfleet established with charter "to boldly go where no man has gone before."

2218 First contact with the Klingon Empire.

2245 Starship *U.S.S. Enterprise* NCC-1701 launched on its first five-year mission under the command of Captain Robert April and First Officer Christopher Pike.

2249 Spock enters Starfleet Academy as the first Vulcan student. Leonard McCoy enters Starfleet Medical School.

2250 James T. Kirk enters Starfleet Academy.

2251 Christopher Pike assumes command of the *Enterprise* for its second five-year mission.

Starfleet Timeline

2252 Spock, still a Starfleet cadet, begins serving under Captain Pike on the *Enterprise*.

2253 Spock graduates from Starfleet Academy. Leonard McCoy graduates from Starfleet Medical School.

2254 James T. Kirk graduates from Starfleet Academy. As a lieutenant, Kirk is assigned duty aboard the *U.S.S. Farragut*.

2261 *U.S.S. Enterprise*, under the command of Captain Christopher Pike, completes its third five-year mission.

2263 James T. Kirk is promoted to captain of the *Enterprise* and meets Christopher Pike, who is promoted to fleet captain.

2264 Captain James T. Kirk, in command of the *U.S.S. Enterprise*, embarks on a historic five-year mission of exploration.

2266 Dr. Leonard McCoy replaces Dr. Mark Piper as chief medical officer aboard the *Enterprise*.

2269 Kirk's original five-year mission ends, and Starship *Enterprise* returns to spacedock. Kirk is promoted to admiral.

Starfleet Timeline

2271 *U.S.S. Enterprise* embarks on Kirk's second five-year mission (*Star Trek: The Motion Picture*).

2277 James T. Kirk accepts a teaching position at Starfleet Academy; Spock assumes command of the Starship *Enterprise*.

2285 In orbit around the Genesis planet, Kirk orders the destruction of the Starship *Enterprise* to prevent the ship from falling into Klingon hands (*Star Trek III: The Search for Spock*).

2286 Kirk is demoted to captain and assigned command of the Starship *Enterprise* NCC-1701-A (*Star Trek IV: The Voyage Home*).

2287 The *Enterprise* is commandeered by Sybok, Spock's half-brother, and taken to the center of the galaxy (*Star Trek V: The Final Frontier*).

2292 Alliance between the Klingon Empire and the Romulan Star Empire collapses.

2293 The Klingon Empire launches a major peace initiative; the crews of the *U.S.S. Enterprise* and the *U.S.S. Excelsior*, captained by Hikaru Sulu, thwart a conspiracy to sabotage the Khitomer Peace Conference. Afterward, the *Enterprise-A* is decommissioned, and Kirk retires from Starfleet.

U.S.S. Enterprise NCC-1701-B, under the command of Captain John Harriman, is severely damaged on her maiden voyage. Honored guest Captain James T. Kirk is listed as missing, presumed killed in action.

2344 *U.S.S. Enterprise* NCC-1701-C, under the command of Captain Rachel Garrett, is destroyed while defending the Klingon outpost on Narendra III from Romulan attack.

2346 Romulan massacre of Klingon outpost on Khitomer.

2364 Captain Jean-Luc Picard assumes command of the *U.S.S. Enterprise* NCC-1701-D.

2367 Borg attack at Wolf 359; *U.S.S. Saratoga* destroyed; First Officer Lieutenant Commander Benjamin Sisko and his son, Jake, are among the survivors; *Enterprise* defeats the Borg vessel in orbit around Earth.

Starfleet Timeline

2369 Commander Benjamin Sisko assumes command of Deep Space Nine in orbit over Bajor.

2371 *U.S.S. Enterprise* NCC-1701-D destroyed on Veridian III.

Former *Enterprise* captain James T. Kirk emerges from a temporal nexus, but dies helping Picard save the Veridian system.

U.S.S. Voyager, under the command of Captain Kathryn Janeway, is accidentally transported to the Delta Quadrant. The crew begins a 70-year journey back to Federation space.

2372 The Klingon Empire's attempted invasion of Cardassia Prime results in the dissolution of the Khitomer peace treaty between the Federation and the Klingon Empire.

Source: *Star Trek® Chronology* / Michael Okuda and Denise Okuda

Chapter
1

Two suns hung low in a turquoise sky. The higher one was a bloated crimson, a squashed red oval that gave little warmth. The lower sun was merely a brilliant point of blue-white light. Across a vast, nearly flat plain of harshly glittering crystalline rock almost exactly the corroded copper-green color of Spock's blood, the horizon became jagged. A range of cobalt-blue volcanic cones thrust their sharp peaks upward, and each mountain cast two sharp-edged shadows on the plain, one shadow a deep violet, the other, paler one, gray green.

Almost directly overhead, an irregular buttery-yellow crescent moon rode waves of crimson, orange, and purple aurora, the shimmering colors as restless as an ocean. Off in the east, a smaller, rounder gray moon had just risen above the roof of the Bel T'aan conference center where fifty diplomats worked to end a war that had gone on for generations. In the darker sky above the sleek building, a few random stars already glittered, their light dimmed in the auroral display. High meteors, their trails brilliant white, scratched across the western sky.

"It is all very—" began Cha-Tuan Mar Lorval, the Marathan youth who had only a few weeks before set foot on his ancestral planet for the first time in his life. The short, stumpy boy hesitated, searching for the right words. "It is very, very—"

"Fascinating," said Spock.

Cha turned his head, his mane of iridescent hair glimmering in the double light of the setting binary suns. "No. I was trying to say *beautiful* but in a more intense way. It is more beautiful than anything I have ever seen." The Marathan boy stole a quick glance back at the Bel T'aan complex, lowered his voice, and murmured, "It is a vision given us by the Ancient Maker."

Spock raised an eyebrow. "The Ancient Maker?"

With an embarrassed shrug, Cha looked away. "I am almost an adult. Such things are forbidden. I cannot speak of them."

"Ah. A religious taboo," Spock said. "I will not question you."

Cha relaxed. "Thank you. But surely even one who is without the knowledge of the Ancient Maker can see the glory, the beauty, of all this."

Spock tilted his head as he considered. The air of Marath was thin and, at this latitude, bitterly cold in his nostrils. He took a deep breath. "The arrangement of the landscape and the placement of astronomical bodies is aesthetically attractive," he admitted. "Though of course it is temporary. The most interesting point for me is the double sun. Marath is one of the few inhabited planets that orbits a double star. Most binary-system planets orbit one of the two suns but not both."

Cha shook his head. "You Vulcans have no soul," he complained. "You're all logic and mathematics and science. You don't appreciate the—the poetry of such a vision." He nodded toward the west. "The larger sun, the reddish one, is Hamarka, the Creator, the one my people call the Ancient Maker. The small, brilliant point of blue-white light, the one that dances around Hamarka, is Volash, the Jester."

Spock nodded. He noted again that he was cold. Marath was not a particularly cold planet—it was even warmer than Vulcan in the lower latitudes—but Bel T'aan, an ancient religious and cultural center, was close to Marath's north pole. After eighteen years of learning Vulcan discipline, though, Spock was used to ignoring mere physical discomfort. "It sounds as if the two suns are part of a myth," he suggested.

"Yes," responded Cha. He shifted his feet, making the short columns of frost crunch and crackle. "I can tell you that. I am not yet of age, and the stories are not part of the True Lore. In the beginning, they were alone; then Volash challenged Hamarka to bring forth some new thing in the universe. It was to be a thing to make them both laugh if Hamarka could do that. Then with a thought, Hamarka created Marath, the world, and all the

3

life upon her, just to amuse the two friends. Is that not a pretty story?"

"It is a standard creation myth," Spock pointed out. Sensing that his observation might create some unfavorable emotion in the other boy, he added, "Although the story is most unusual in its assumption that the universe was created as a—we have no Vulcan term for the concept, but an Earth word is *joke*."

Cha walked a few meters away, leaving a trail of dark footprints against the frost, and sat on a rounded boulder. He huddled into his heavy jacket, for even to someone whose ancestors came from Marath, the afternoon was growing uncomfortably chilly. Already the distant blue volcanoes had begun to show long jagged streaks of white frost. "It is a bitter joke," he said softly. "A joke that drove my people away from our home world in the time of my great-grandfather's father's great-grandfathers."

Marathans had a curious way of measuring historical periods. Spock looked at his friend. They had only met a few weeks ago, but they had learned they could talk easily to one another. Cha's father, Karos Mar Santor, was a diplomatic assistant in the Shakir mission to the home world. Since Spock's father, Sarek, was an accomplished diplomat himself, the two young men had much in common. Spock had no doubt that Sarek would succeed in drawing the three factions together, for his father had infinite patience and a gift for directing negotiations in the most logical channels.

Still, the problem was complex and delicate. Marath,

4

the planet on which Spock and Cha stood, was the second world from the binary star in a seven-planet system. For many centuries, different nations had existed on Marath, almost always at war. The constant warfare had many causes: struggles for territory, struggles for power, even conflicts over points of religion. More than five hundred years earlier, scientists on Marath, working to create new and terrible weapons, had developed space flight. The weapon became a means of escape when a fierce global war broke out. Outcasts from the home world of Marath settled first two moons of Gandar, the third planet in the system. Gandar was a swollen gas giant with eleven major moons, two of them large enough to support life. Another group of refugees sheltered on distant Shakir, the fourth world in the system, a planet almost inhospitably cold, except for its equatorial region. Shakir was Cha's home.

And now that scientists on Shakir had developed a primitive form of warp drive, they had encountered hostile Klingons uncomfortably close to them in space. Suddenly all the enemy factions in the system had a new foe to dread. The Marathan system had applied to become part of the United Federation of Planets. The Federation was willing, but only if the Marathans could finally resolve their old hostilities. Sarek had launched the historic peace effort that now, after three years of diplomatic struggle, was finally on the verge of producing a treaty—and, everyone hoped, a lasting peace.

Cha turned to say something to Spock, blinked, and gestured toward the conference center. "Look!"

Spock glanced over his left shoulder and noted that all the lights were on—every light inside and outside the building shone with a clear white glare. "They have achieved accord," he murmured. "The agreement has been reached."

Cha came to stand beside Spock. "Yes," he said, his voice surprisingly tense.

Raising an eyebrow, Spock studied Cha's profile. The Marathan teen's features showed no pleasure. They were set in a scowl of—discontent? Anger? Emotions were so hard to read, thought Spock. Especially the emotions of aliens. "I wish you satisfaction in the agreement," Spock said.

Cha did not look at him. "We'd better go in," he said.

The warmth of the conference center was welcome after the chilly afternoon. An aide offered both Spock and Cha a tall tubular glass with a few centimeters of *tshak,* a hot Marathan drink. They accepted and quickly gulped the fiery orange liquid, as was polite. It tasted both sweet and bitter, and the spices in it were surprisingly hot. As the steaming drink warmed him from inside, Spock looked around. Dozens of people stood in the grand hall, clustered in groups of six or seven. At last Spock saw his father, Sarek, at the center of one of these groups.

The tall, dignified Vulcan towered above the stocky Marathans around him. As the two boys maneuvered toward him, Spock noticed that one of the Marathans standing near Sarek was Cha's father, Karos Mar Santor. Like his son, Karos looked tense and unhappy. His mane of hair, even more impressive than his son's, had lost some of its luster, and the rainbow colors were muted, but Karos was a healthy, vigorous man. As he spoke to Sarek, he gave the impression of great energy under weak control. Spock wondered what emotion Karos felt. Was the word *angry?* Or was it a different feeling? Spock could only guess.

Sarek nodded a greeting as Spock and Cha drew near. "Welcome, my son. Good afternoon, young Mar."

Cha murmured some pleasantry and then spoke to his own father: "Well?"

"The majority have approved a treaty," Karos said shortly, his voice harsh, rasping. "We will not speak of it now."

"But, Father—"

"We will talk of it later!" snapped Karos.

The abruptness of Karos's manner surprised Spock. Like his son, Karos was an easygoing, humorous individual. True, Spock had come to realize that even a being who enjoyed laughter could be very serious indeed when dealing with matters of importance. And it was equally true that the negotiations had lasted for a long time and had been most demanding. And yet . . .

And yet something more was wrong. Spock could sense it in the tension between father and son, in the hopeless but determined glare Cha gave the older Marathan, in the way they both turned abruptly and walked away.

Spock moved to his father's side. "Have you reached a satisfactory accord?"

Sarek replied, "We have at least forged a treaty. It recognizes the unity of the Marathan peoples but grants sovereignty to each group. No side is completely satisfied with it."

"Then it is not a good treaty?"

Sarek gave his son a considering look, the faintest hint of warmth in his eyes. "On the contrary, Spock. The best treaty always leaves every party a little unsatisfied, because all must surrender something of importance in order for the whole group to gain."

"I will remember that." The groups had rearranged themselves, with heated but quiet conversations going on all around the room. Outside both suns had set, and the sky had grown quite dark. Marath was near a cluster of bright stars, or rather was within a few dozen light-years of them, and some were so brilliant that Spock could see them through the glass windows, even with the interior of the conference center radiant with light. In a far corner, Cha and his father had joined a group of negotiators from Shakir, the cold outpost of the Marathan civilization. They kept looking Sarek's way, and none of the looks were friendly. One of them, a grim-looking elderly Marathan whose hair had faded to silvery blue, turned his craggy, wrinkled face toward the two Vulcans and scowled at them. The hum and murmur of conversation were urgent and low. "Father," Spock said, "the Shakir delegation appears to have strong reservations about the treaty."

"Yes," responded Sarek with a sigh. "The old man is Hul Minak Lasvor, a rebel leader in the space war fought between Shakir and Marath thirty years ago. He was opposed to any agreement, and in some ways, the other members of the Shakir delegation agreed with him. They wished to include some concessions that the Marathan delegation refused, chiefly having to do with rights of passage to and from the home world. It was a serious block to negotiation, and at last I was able to overcome it only by specifying in the treaty that such questions will be resolved through more negotiations over the next ten standard years." After a pause, Sarek added, "I do not fully understand the heat with which the diplomats argued this problem. Strong emotions enter into it, and the Marathans are most reluctant to explain their reasons to an outsider."

"I have noticed that, Father." The two Vulcans were walking toward a bank of turbolifts that would take them to their quarters. "Still, a treaty of any sort will help the Marathans in their application to join the Federation, will it not?"

They stepped into the turbolift, and Sarek said, "Habitation level, diplomatic guest quarters one." To Spock he said, "The treaty will do much more than that, my son. You must understand what has happened here. Thanks to diplomacy, the system has avoided bloodshed and war. That is an accomplishment of great merit in itself. And perhaps they have taken a first step, a small step, toward becoming truly one people. That is an even greater accomplishment. Do you understand me?"

The turbolift sighed to a stop, and father and son got out. The corridor into which they stepped was softly lit, arched, and silent. They walked toward their rooms as Spock slowly answered, "I believe I do understand, Father. You have taught the Marathans the value of diplomacy, the logic of settling their disputes bloodlessly. You have given them a start on the path to full civilization."

"Not I," Sarek gently corrected his son. "The Vulcan way of logic. I am only the instrument of logic on Marath. Spock, I want you to consider how rare logic is in the universe. Our scientists believe there are hundreds of thousands, perhaps millions, of sentient races in the galaxy. What is the norm among them? War, hatred, bigotry, force. What is the greatest good we can do for them? To teach them there is a way out: the way our forebears discovered in the control of emotion and the use of logic."

The door sensed their approach, identified them as the occupants of the rooms it guarded, and silently opened for them. They stepped inside, and the lights immediately came on. Spock said slowly, "Yes, Father. I understand."

"Good." Sarek sighed. "I know your gifts, Spock. You wish to be a scientist, and you have won a great honor in being admitted to the Science Academy on Vulcan. However, remember that a good diplomat may also be a good scientist. The universe is full of warring peoples, and many of them live in planets that our science has neither discovered nor described."

After a moment of silence, Spock said, "Are we to return home now, Father?"

The way Sarek looked at him might have made a

human teen anxious, for it was a glance that clearly said Sarek had grasped Spock's strong desire to change the subject. But Spock was only half human, and his Vulcan side enabled him to do away with anxiety. Well, almost.

Sarek said, "Yes, now we will prepare to return home. The treaty will not be official until transmission to the United Federation of Planets for archiving and verification. The little work that remains can be done by subspace communication. We must prepare to leave tomorrow."

"Tomorrow?" Spock asked, not managing to hide the surprise in his voice. "So soon?"

"Yes. A Federation ship has entered orbit around Marath, and it will transport the Marathan off-worlders to their own homes. It will also take us to Vulcan, so we need not call for a Vulcan ship."

"I see. And what is the ship?" asked Spock.

"I did not make a point of asking its name. A ship is a ship," replied Sarek. After a moment, he said, "Though now that I think of it, I did overhear some Marathans speaking of it. I believe the ship we are to take is called . . . *Enterprise.*"

Chapter 2

The cloud-streaked turquoise sky, the level plain, the misty distant blue volcanoes of Marath shimmered away, and a moment later, a dim, cool cubicle shimmered into existence. Sarek stepped down from the transporter platform, and Spock followed him. A young human man, dressed in the greenish-gold tunic of a Starfleet command officer, left the console from which he had operated the transporter controls. "Ambassador Sarek, Mr. Spock, welcome aboard the *Enterprise.* I am First Officer Christopher Pike. The captain will be pleased to see you."

Sarek inclined his head. "And I to see him. Thank you, Lieutenant Commander Pike."

"Captain April wanted me to show you to your quarters," Pike said. "He thought you might want to accustom yourselves to our gravity and atmosphere for an hour or so. He will meet you at eleven hundred if that is agreeable."

"Certainly," Sarek said.

They left the transporter room and walked down a curving corridor. The first thing Spock noticed was the gravity, lighter than that of Marath, far lighter than that of Vulcan. He moved carefully, accustoming himself to his new weight. Crew members, men and women, hurried past them, giving them inquisitive but friendly glances as they passed. "I understand that congratulations are in order for young Spock," Pike said as they took the lift to the accommodations deck. "It isn't every eighteen-year-old Vulcan who receives an unconditional appointment to the Vulcan Science Academy."

Spock gravely inclined his head. "Thank you, Lieutenant Commander Pike. I did not realize my acceptance was news."

"Oh, certainly," Pike said. "Your father is a gifted diplomat, and those of us in Starfleet are grateful to him. The Marathan system is a real weak spot in our border with the Klingon Empire, and Sarek's work will make the Federation much more secure. Naturally we're interested in all the news about him—and in his son. You must be excited about attending the Science Academy."

"No," Spock said honestly. "I am—gratified but not excited."

"Of course," Pike said with a grin. "Excitement is a human emotion. I forgot for a second. Well, here you are: adjoining cabins. Your luggage has already been brought here. I'm afraid it's a little plain, but the *Enter-*

prise has been called on to fight battles more than to transport honored guests. I hope these will be all right."

"They fulfill their function admirably," Sarek said. "Thank you, Lieutenant Commander Pike."

"You're quite welcome." Pike indicated a wall-mounted device. "If you wish to set the environmental controls to something more like a Vulcan atmosphere, just call Engineering on the intership communicator here. I will come for you shortly before eleven hundred hours and escort you to the captain's conference room."

"Thank you. I shall use the interval to meditate."

As Pike turned to leave, Spock said, "Father? May I see the ship?"

Sarek replied, "That is up to Lieutenant Commander Pike."

"Sure," Pike said. "Come along."

As they walked along the curving corridor, Spock breathed deeply and looked around. The atmosphere was ideal for a human crew, but to someone used to the thin air of Vulcan, it was incredibly rich with aromas: lubricants, faint hints of protein and fruit as they passed a dining area, undertones of minerals, and a strong tang of oxygen.

"Like to see the engine room?" asked Pike.

"That would be most gratifying," Spock returned.

Their tour started there. Assistant Engineer Welborne welcomed them; showed them the dilithium containment chambers, the reactor coils, and the power controls; and explained about Cochrane warp generators. Spock listened politely, never once indicating that he knew all

1 5

about these rather elementary processes. Pike then took him to the xenobiology labs, the sensor control center, and finally suggested returning to the transporter room. "The Marathans are coming aboard," he explained. "We're giving some of them a lift to their home worlds. I think we'll just have time to see them aboard before your father has his appointment with Captain April."

They returned to the same transporter room where Spock and Sarek had beamed aboard. Pike took his position behind the control console and explained the principles behind the matter-transport device. "I understand that Vulcan scientists have helped to refine this invention," he said as he finished.

Spock nodded. "Yes, the biological pattern buffer has been made much more reliable thanks to Sunok of Vulcan. Prior to his invention, the transporter was only 99.9992 percent accurate in transporting living subjects. Thanks to Sunok's incorporation of Vulcan uncertainty physics, it is now virtually impossible for the device to malfunction—from a purely physical perspective, I mean. There is always human error."

"Hey," laughed Pike.

Spock gave him an inquisitive look. "Forgive me. Of course I should have said *operator* error. The species of the operator is immaterial to the point. It was thoughtless of me."

"No offense taken," Pike said.

At that moment, the intercom came to life: "*Enterprise,* the Marathan delegates are ready to come aboard. Twenty-four to beam up."

"We will take them in groups of six," Pike responded. "First group, stand by." He adjusted the controls. "Energizing."

Spoke watched as bands of Marathans came twinkling into existence on the transporter pad. Cha was in the third group, and he made his way over as soon as he stepped off the pad. "Hello, Spock." His voice was low, guarded.

"Hello, Cha."

"Well," Cha said with a nervous smile, "at least you'll get to see my home."

"I look forward to that."

Crew members had come to show the Marathans to their quarters. They were a silent group, and Spock realized that something was not right. None of them looked around at the starship or its crew. None showed the least interest in their surroundings. And, except for Cha, no one spoke.

As for Cha, he muttered quick, meaningless observations—"Very warm air, isn't it? Wonder where that goes?"—that called for no response.

In a low voice, Spock said, "Forgive me, Cha, but what is wrong?"

Cha gave him a quick glance, his iridescent hair glittering electric blue, magenta, yellow. "Wrong? I don't know what you mean, Spock."

"You don't seem yourself."

"Cha!" It was the loud voice of Karos Mar Santor, Cha's father. "Come. Here are our quarters."

Cha hurried away, not even looking back. The door

1 7

hissed open, the Marathan father and son entered their quarters, and the door closed again.

"We just have time to escort your father to the captain's conference room," Pike said. Spock followed him, still wondering about the transformation that had come over Cha. It was—disturbing.

Pike led Sarek and Spock to the conference room, where the tall, craggy Captain Robert April welcomed them with a smile. He turned to Pike and said, "Lieutenant Commander, report to the bridge and take us out of orbit. Set a course for Gandar, standard impulse."

"Yes, Captain," Pike said. "Permission to allow Mr. Spock on the bridge?"

Captain April raised his eyebrows. "Granted. Enjoy yourself, Mr. Spock."

Spock did not point out that Vulcans did not enjoy themselves. He was too filled with anticipation—a sensation, he thought fleetingly, that in some ways almost resembled excitement. He followed Pike into the turbolift, where Pike ordered, "Bridge." To Spock, Pike added, "Don't expect anything spectacular. You won't even feel anything when we leave orbit, although you'll get a good view of Marath from where we are."

"I understand," Spock said.

They stepped from the lift onto the bridge. Spock quickly took it all in: a large circular room, the forewall dominated by an enormous viewscreen. At the moment, the green-, blue-, purple-, and white-streaked world of Marath rotated there, huge in the viewscreen, with a clear band of twilight separating the night side from the

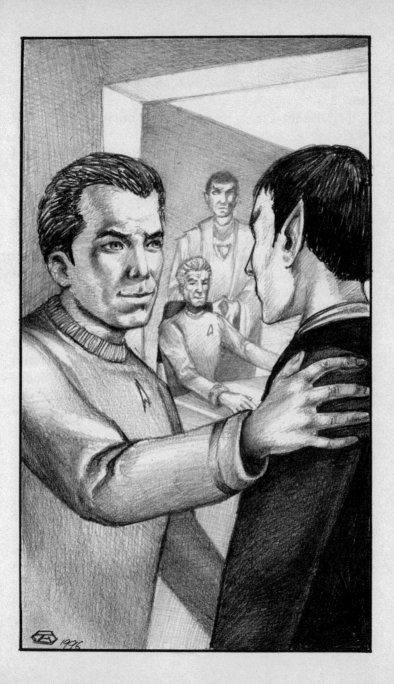

day side. That, of course, was the effect of the binary sun.

"Mr. Bann, I'm here to take us out of orbit," said Pike.

The helmsman, a completely bald young man, glanced over his shoulder. "Aye-aye, sir."

Pike settled into the captain's seat. "We have a visitor on the bridge," he announced. "This is Mr. Spock. Spock, the lieutenant in the driver's seat is Ledrick Bann; our navigator is Selena Niles; at communications is Lieutenant Michael Daron; our science officer is Lieutenant Richard Cheyney; and the grumpy old man at the engineering station is Chief Engineer Powell."

Spock nodded to each in turn. "Lieutenant Cheyney, may I join you?" he asked.

"Sure," said Cheyney, a strongly built young human with a closely cut crop of red hair. Spock went to stand slightly behind him, marveling at the compact science center. "If you want to know what anything's for, just ask," Cheyney said. "It's really pretty quiet now. I'm just monitoring our status, that's all."

"Thank you."

"Computer," said Cheyney, "show us a schematic of the primary stars in this system."

"Working," the computer said in its mechanical, but strangely feminine, voice. A moment later, one of the display panels lit with a representation of the two suns, the crushed oval of the red giant, the brilliant blue pinhead of the fierce companion. Swirls of gas connected them.

"Fascinating," Spock said. "A binary system that has remained stable for more than three billion years."

"It's the strange composition of the blue-white companion that does it," Cheyney replied. "It takes up just enough cast-off matter from the companion giant to compensate for its own rate of reaction. Most binaries in this configuration are doomed to a few million years of existence at best, but the Marathan system's good for another four billion years or so."

"Four billion three hundred and seventy-one million nine thousand six hundred and three," Spock replied.

Catching Cheyney's surprised look, he added, "Assuming a uniform rate of matter loss, of course."

"Oh, of course," Cheyney said with a grin.

Behind them, Christopher Pike had ordered a course laid in for Gandar, the next planet out in the system. As soon as the navigation station reported the course laid in, Pike ordered, "Take us out of orbit, Helmsman. Ahead standard impulse power."

"Ahead standard impulse," repeated Lieutenant Bann, and Spock turned to watch.

In the view screen, Marath sank away and out of sight. The stars wheeled as the *Enterprise* changed course. Then, as the stars stabilized, a brilliant orange point of light glowed in the center of the screen. "Increase magnification by a factor of ten," ordered Pike.

The image changed. Now Spock saw an orange disk, streaked with reds and swirled with yellows. Around it hung seven, no, eight smaller disks, the principal moons of Gandar. The other three moons were too small to see at this distance. "Estimated arrival in thirty-one hours," the navigator said.

"Very good. Maintain course and power."

Spock took a deep breath. On their trip to Marath, aboard a severely practical Vulcan transport ship, he had seen nothing like this. Vulcan ships depended on mathematical displays, not visual representations of the universe. This way, the human way, was much more, well, fascinating.

After an hour, he returned to his quarters, still mulling over what he had seen and experienced. Sarek was in the common sitting area they shared, reading from a compact book display screen. "Well," he said, "the crew of this ship is certainly considerate of you."

"Yes, Father," Spock returned. "The bridge is most interesting."

Sarek set the book down, tented his fingers, and stared over them at his son. "Spock," he said, "a word of warning. You are still young, and you have a human side to control. Please remember that enthusiasm is an emotion. It is unseemly."

Spock returned his father's gaze. Sarek ignored him, picked up his book, and began to read again. On stiff legs, Spock walked into his bedroom, the door hissing closed behind him.

He felt—if he had been human, he *would* have felt—an emotion and a strong one.

It was shame.

Chapter
3

Gandar was huge and terrible in the viewscreen, its gaseous surface whipped by hydrogen winds rushing at hundreds of kilometers per hour. Along the night terminator, branches of lightning forked and sputtered, some so long that on Vulcan they would have reached from one hemisphere of the planet halfway around the other. At the poles, coronas of electromagnetic energy pulsed and glowed a hundred colors, all shades of red, blue, violet, green, and yellow.

Watching the chaotic surface, which moved visibly—the enormous planet spun on its poles every 8.3 hours, giving it days and nights just over four hours long each—Spock wondered what it would be like to live on either of the two habitable moons. The moons were both in tidal lock, with one face forever toward the gas giant, the other eternally facing space. Anyone on the inner hemisphere would always see that vast orange sphere hanging overhead, day or night, taking up half the sky, seeming almost close enough to touch. It must be oppressive, Spock thought. It would be like waiting for the sky to fall.

The innermost moon, Fleta, whirled around the giant planet in a complete orbit every eight days. Unlike its primary, Fleta had a night four days long and then another variable one when it plunged into Gandar's deep shadow. Fortunately, the gas giant, too small to be a real star, still had enough reaction heat to warm the little moon. The other inhabited moon, Jareta, was farther out, in a three-week orbit. It was also colder, and the Marathans who disembarked there beamed down wearing enviro suits that provided precious warmth. Jareta's space-facing hemisphere was too cold for habitation, so all the colonists lived on the planet side.

And once they had gone, only the half-dozen representatives of Shakir remained in the Marathan quarters. Spock saw little of them. Cha had retreated from friendship and was distant and cool whenever Spock saw him. The adults—including the aged and grim Hul Minak Lasvor—gave Spock even less notice. Once Spock and Sarek, on their way to an observation deck, met Minak coming the other way. The old Marathan glowered at them, his eyes flashing. Sarek inclined his head politely. "Live long and prosper, Ambassador Minak," he murmured.

"We know what you have done," Minak said, and he swept past them.

Spock looked after him. "What did he mean, Father?"

Sarek took some moments before replying. "The Shakir colonists are the most bitter," he said at last. "A religious war forced them off the planet more than two hundred years ago. Shakir is a hard environment, bitterly cold except in one narrow habitable band. Hul Minak Lasvor leads a faction that wishes to retake Marath itself, to impose order and enforce obedience to the Shakirian branch of their faith on the home world."

"Impossible," Spock said at once. "Their numbers are far too small."

"Dreams of glory die hard, my son. And when those dreams turn bitter, they lead to thoughts of tyranny and revenge."

They spoke no more of it. But a few days later, when the *Enterprise* went into orbit around the inhospitable planet Shakir, Spock remembered his father's words.

Shakir was a gloomy reddish-purple sphere, its rocky surface splotched with frozen hydrocarbons and water ice. Cratered and ancient, even its sunward face looked dark, forbidding. The planet had one redeeming feature: Unlike Vulcan or Earth, which inclined on their poles relative to their suns, Shakir's north and south poles were almost exactly vertical with regard to the binary sun.

The planet had no seasons at all. But because the warmth was constant, it did have a narrow green band around its equator only several hundred kilometers broad. Here liquid water existed (barely; night temperatures invariably were below freezing), and tough, hardy plant life grew in abundance. Here, too, the Marathan colonists had dug in, fashioning underground homes, complexes of tunnels. And here they led molelike existences, buried underground but dreaming of the stars.

"Farewell, Cha," Spock said as he stood beside Lieutenant Commander Pike.

On the transporter pad, Cha glanced at his father and then barely nodded. His face was blank, expressionless.

"Energize," said Hul Minak Lasvor, his voice cold.

"Energizing," responded Pike. He adjusted the controls, the transporter gave its peculiar musical hum, and the last six Marathans beamed off the ship.

"Well," said Pike. "That's done. Are you busy, Spock?"

"No. I have nothing to do at the moment."

"Then come with me, and we'll drop into the junior officers' wardroom. We senior officers like to eat with them from time to time. A glimpse of our splendor encourages them to do their best and become worthy of promotion."

"Really?"

Pike laughed at Spock's quizzical expression. "No. A joke. But it is an old service tradition, and the junior officers invited me today. They'll be glad to have you join them as well."

"A joke," Spock said thoughtfully. "I know the concept of humor, but what is its purpose?"

With a shrug, Pike said, "To relieve stress, I suppose."

"Did beaming the Marathans down cause you stress?"

Pike led the way into the corridor. "Beaming them down didn't, but perhaps having them aboard did. We tried to be as hospitable as possible. Hul Minak Lasvor even got an in-depth inspection of the Computer and Engineering sections. But they weren't cheerful guests."

"No," agreed Spock.

The wardroom was a narrow, curving compartment with four tables, each one with four to six young men and women already seated. They welcomed the newcomers, and Pike himself brought Spock's vegetarian lunch to the table. Spock was quiet as he ate, listening to the exchanges between the young Starfleet officers with interest. Much was technical—a discussion of some minor computer problems that had just appeared, from what Spock gathered—and much was humorous. The cadets, ensigns, and lieutenants all seemed to be enjoying their lives immensely.

At the end of the meal, the bald helmsman, Lieutenant Bann, called out to Spock from the next table: "Stick around. You can see me teach this young upstart from Engineering a lesson in three-dimensional chess."

Spock turned to Pike. "May I?"

"By all means," said Pike, gesturing Spock toward the table. "Are you a chess aficionado, Mr. Spock?"

"I am not. I do not know what chess is. But I am interested."

"Oh, well, come on," said Bann, grinning. He and the others had cleared the table and had set up something resembling an abstract sculpture, a kind of branching structure with flat rectangles here and there, the rectangles divided into brown and ivory squares. As he set silver and ebony figures on this device, Bann said, "Mr.

Spock, I don't think you've met Ensign Thedra Alfort. Thedra, Spock is the son of Sarek, the Vulcan ambassador who arranged the Marathan treaty."

Thedra Alfort was a young human female with short black hair, startling blue eyes, and a quizzical expression. She nodded to Spock. "How do you do?"

Spock knew enough about human speech not to ask, "How do I do what?" He merely nodded gravely in response. "You are an engineer?" he asked.

"One day I may be," Thedra said with a wry grin. "Right now I'm desperately trying to learn."

Bann held out his clenched hands. "Choose."

Thedra tapped his right hand, and he opened it to reveal a silver figurine. "You go first." He put the silver chessman and an ebony one matching it on the board. To Spock, he said, "I'm the chess champion of the *Enterprise*. Thedra has rashly decided to challenge me."

"Ah," said Spock. "It is a contest."

"A contest of wit and intelligence," agreed Bann. "As we play, I'll explain how each piece moves. Maybe you'd like to learn the game."

Spock watched as Thedra went down to long, hard-fought defeat. For most of an hour she held her own or was down only a pawn or so. But Bann had an uncanny knack of anticipating her moves, blocking her plans, and retaliating in unexpected ways. Finally, her king trapped and one rook just taken by a bishop, Thedra shook her head. "No use," she sighed. "It would be mate in four moves. I resign."

"Mate in three moves," responded Bann with a grin. "But hey, who's counting?"

The young officers had formed a circle around the two, and throughout play they had murmured observations and comments. Now they commiserated with Thedra. "Hey, don't take it so hard," one said. "He beat me in fifteen minutes flat!"

Another punched the speaker playfully on the arm. "And that was no great feat either."

"May I play?" Spock asked.

They all fell silent, giving him surprised glances.

Bann looked up, his bald head glistening. "Are you serious?"

Spock raised an eyebrow. "Yes."

With a sharklike grin, Bann began to set up the board. "This I have to see," he announced. "Have a seat, my Vulcan friend."

"Half Vulcan," Spock responded, sitting across the board from Bann.

Bann paused in setting up the pawns. "Really?"

"My mother is human," explained Spock.

Bann's grin became more friendly. "My father is, too," he said. "My mother's Deltan, though. Well, as one half human to another, good luck."

"Chance does not appear to play a great role in this contest," Spock observed.

With a laugh, Bann said, "You take the silver pieces as a courtesy to a new player. Let the slaughter begin!"

The officers crowded around as Spock made his first move. Lieutenant Bann nodded. "A standard gambit," he said, "which I counter like this." He moved a pawn.

With Spock's next move, a murmur began. Then when he moved again, it became a buzz. Bann frowned at the board, reached to move a knight, thought better of it, and instead castled his king. Spock responded by taking a bishop. "I didn't see *that* coming," someone said.

"Shh," hissed Bann, scowling in concentration.

Three more exchanges of moves, and then Spock sent

his rook down to his opponent's level. "I will capture your king with the next move," he said.

Bann exhaled. "You say, 'Checkmate' now.'

"Why do I say that?"

"Because you beat me, that's why."

"Oh. Checkmate."

"Eleven minutes and nineteen seconds," someone said, awe in her voice. "I never thought it was possible."

"You've played before," Bann said to Spock.

"No, I haven't."

"Come on. How could you beat me if you've never played the game?"

Spock looked up. He was the center of attention. "It is a very logical process," he said simply.

They all laughed as if he had made a joke. Even Bann grinned. "Spock, I met you two years too late. If I'd only known you during my senior year at Starfleet Academy, you could have tutored me in logic. Then maybe I could have done better in Fedderling's class and graduated first instead of ninth!"

"Fedderling's a terror," Thedra Alfort agreed. "Wouldn't it be great to see him arguing with someone as logical as Spock?"

A muscular lieutenant in a red Security tunic chuckled. "I'd give up two years seniority to see that," he said.

"Hey," someone else said, "Fedderling's class was no joke, but what about the simulator trials? Can't you just see Spock at the control when old Jeffries causes three simultaneous systems failures? Zip! Zap! Zowie! 'The repairs were all very logical, Mr. Jeffries!' "

Spock said mildly, "I do not understand what—"

A razzing klaxon horn cut him off. The young officers leaped toward the door, and Spock found himself trotting along the corridor beside Mr. Bann. "What is happening?" he asked.

Without looking around, the young lieutenant snapped, "We must be under attack. It's a red alert!"

Chapter 4

Spock stepped off the turbolift and stood to one side as Lieutenant Bann relieved an ensign at the helm. Captain April sat in the command seat, his back to Spock, his attention riveted to the viewscreen. And on the screen, a stocky, grim-faced Marathan—Karos Mar Santor, Spock noted, Cha's father—was speaking: "—are completely surrounded, Captain April, and helpless. We are not pirates. We do not seek to rob you, only to prevent great harm to our own people. We want only the certified original of the Marathan treaty created by the spy Sarek. If you surrender that, you will be free to go."

April's voice was harsh and icy: "This is an outrage, Mar. Sarek is no spy. He's a decorated ambassador, and you yourself agreed to the treaty."

The Marathan suddenly looked old and weary, but his tone did not change: "That does not matter now. I tell you, Hul Minak Lasvor's rebel fighters will take the treaty by force if they must. The rest of us have no control over him. It was only through the utmost persuasion that we convinced him to allow us to give you this warning. Surrender the spy Sarek and the draft of the treaty, Captain April, and avoid an unnecessary confrontation."

April shook his head. "This is a grave violation of interstellar law. If Marath truly wants to join the Federation, this is a strange way of going about it!"

Mar said, "Perhaps all of Marath does not want to join the Federation. And if the original draft of the treaty is not transported to Federation headquarters, it never will."

Captain April's voice became a bit more conciliatory. "Look, Mar, I don't know why you've made this senseless demand. The treaty is not final yet anyway. Whatever your objections are, you have time yet to address them, to correct any errors. You have weeks of negotiations by subspace communication to put the finishing details—"

The Marathan looked sick, anguished. His voice sounded choked as he muttered, "I cannot explain our actions. It is forbidden to speak of such things to outsiders, but please believe me, Captain April, we are well aware of the state of the treaty and of the negotiations still to be done. None of that matters now."

April was silent for a long moment. "Very well. Let me warn you, though, the *Enterprise* is well equipped to defend herself against any attack by Marathan fighters.

Let your rebel leader know that aggression against a Federation vessel is a serious mistake."

"This is pointless," said Mar. "Captain April, you will transport the official copy of the treaty to the coordinates I will transmit. Ambassador Sarek must be turned over to the Marathan government in exile in Shakir for trial. You have one *qual.* At the end of that time, if you have not surrendered the draft of the treaty and the ambassador, Minak will take both by force." The screen blanked, and a second later, it resolved into a starfield.

"A *qual,*" said Lieutenant Commander Pike, "is just over seventeen standard minutes. Not much time."

April stared at the viewscreen. It showed white streaks against the star-spattered blackness of space, inconsiderable silvery scratches on a vast, dark background. "There they are. Can you imagine them trying to stand up against our firepower? Sensor report: How many enemy craft?"

"Thirty-one," the science officer, Lieutenant Cheyney, said promptly. "They are all single-pilot attack vessels, capable of light speed. I have one isolated. Shall I put it on screen?"

"Yes," Captain April said. "Maximum magnification."

The viewscreen wavered, then refocused on a streaking silver form. It was delta shaped, a silver triangle pivoting against the darkness of space, and moving fast relative to the stationary background of stars. There was no way of telling how large—or small—it was with nothing to compare it to. The science officer seemed to sense that and, consulting his instruments, said, "It is approximately 3.47 meters long with a span of 5.2 meters at its broadest part. The power plant is a Marathan impulse engine, with a secondary warp nacelle using matter–antimatter flux. It is armed with one laser cannon and three neutron torpedoes."

"Hopeless," April said, shaking his head. "Ants attacking a giant. Raise shields, Mr. Belas."

"Aye, Captain." This came from the security station, but a second later, the burly lieutenant manning the console said, "Sir, the shields aren't responding."

April turned in his seat. "Chief Engineer Powell, get on that. Mr. Belas, arm laser cannon and photon torpedoes."

"Weapons systems are not responding either" the lieutenant reported. "Sir, our defensive and offensive systems are dead in the water."

"Take us to warp four."

"I can't," Chief Engineer Powell said tightly, working frantically at his station. His seamed face wore an expression of anger and frustration. "We've got serious problems here, too."

"Sir," said the young science officer, "without shields, the neutron torpedoes can destroy all life aboard the ship, while leaving the physical structures intact."

"I'm well aware of that, Mr. Cheyney," growled April. "Number one, how's our time?"

"We have 14.5 minutes left, sir."

April swiveled back. "What's wrong with the computers, Mr. Cheyney?"

The science officer was frantically scanning readouts.

"Sabotage, sir. Someone evidently used a master override device, an isolinear command unit, to alter our security codes. Nothing in the defense or weapons programs is making sense."

"Solve the problem."

"Aye, sir, but the mathematics is all wrong. It seems to be base four, but—"

"Chief Engineer, what about warp speed?"

Powell turned from his console, and when he spoke, his voice was furious but controlled: "Sir, the field damping system is not on-line. We could conceivably go to warp, but it wouldn't be pleasant, especially with those thirty shielded fighters so close around us."

"What would happen?"

The chief engineer rapidly made some calculations. "The warp field would be thrown in flux. There's a better than even chance that the warp cores would break down under the strain. And we'd certainly drag a third or more of those ships with us. Their pilots would be dead for sure. Most likely their antimatter containment fields would collapse, and the *Enterprise* herself could blow up within thirty seconds of engaging warp drive."

"What's the risk of a core breakdown?" asked the captain.

Chief Engineer Powell shook his head. "I'd say roughly seventy percent."

"Seventy-one point three eight seven percent," Spock corrected. "That is a closer approximation."

April turned and glared at him. "What's this civilian doing on my bridge?"

"I will leave if you wish," Spock said. "However, I believe I may be of use. I have some experience with computer languages, and I may be able to repair your problem."

"Sir," Pike said, "nine minutes left. Mr. Spock is an extremely gifted young man. It couldn't hurt to let him have a try."

"Very well, Mr. Spock. Take the science officer's console," April said.

Spock joined Science Officer Cheyney. "The key," he said, "is that base four mathematical structure you mentioned. It is typical of Marathan computer language unlike your own binary code. May I?" Richard Cheyney, his lean face drawn even tighter by tension, nodded and made room for Spock. The young Vulcan's thin fingers flew over the console, calling up a dizzying array of symbols and numbers.

"Sir," said the communications officer, "the fighters are in close containment configuration around the ship. We're completely surrounded. I'm putting the enemy vessels on screen."

Spock barely glanced around. His one look told him what he already sensed: The thirty-one Marathan fighters were in tight, angry orbits around the *Enterprise*, a whirling cloud of gnats around the great starship. Alone, each would be negligible. Even a fully armed fighter could do only minimal damage to the Federation ship, perhaps breaching the hull in one or two places, perhaps killing a few dozen of its crew. But concentrated, directed fire from thirty-one laser cannons could easily disable the *Enterprise*'s unshielded engines, and more than ninety neutron torpedoes, evenly scattered, would instantly kill every life form aboard the ship, leaving everything else intact. Spock concentrated on the computer display. He caught two lines of mathematical symbols, erased them, and replaced them with a quick formula of his own devising.

"Ah," he said. "Try to raise the shields now."

"Shields coming up," reported the weapons officer, relief in his voice. "Power is rising slowly. Ten percent. Fifteen. Twenty-three. Thirty ... Thirty-three percent strength and holding."

"Shield power is steady," confirmed Chief Engineer Powell. "It's still only one feed, though, so we can't bring shields to full. I could try diverting more power to the shields from life support, but that's going to require routing around the sabotaged systems. I can't get shields to fifty percent for another ten minutes, unless we have a miracle."

"Thirty percent is barely enough to protect us from the laser fire," said April. "But the torpedoes would get through. Spock, see if you can give us weapons control."

"I am working on it."

"Six minutes," said Pike. "Sir, the enemy ships have detected our shields. They're moving into a tighter pattern."

"Hold her steady as she goes," April commanded.

"Aye, sir," said Lieutenant Bann. "Steady as she goes."

"How are you doing?" asked Cheyney anxiously.

"It is difficult," Spock responded. "The computer language in nine different subroutines has been reset to the base four system, but in addition, the programs have been encoded. I suspect there is an encryption key, a code word, that I do not know. Perhaps if I routed the patterns through the universal translator array, I could grasp the key word required to free the system."

Spock adjusted the controls, and a rolling yellow column of Marathan words, rendered in the elegant curves of Vulcan script, began to scroll upward on one screen so fast that to human eyes they were hardly more than a blur. The science officer reached to touch a control, but Spock grasped his wrist, preventing the change. "It is not necessary to slow the display," he explained. "I can read very rapidly."

"Five minutes," said Pike.

Spock tried several Marathan phrases and expressions, but none of them unlocked the sealed programs. The column of words continued to flash by on the screen.

"Three minutes," warned Pike.

"Send a Security team to Ambassador Sarek's quarters," ordered Captain April. "They may attempt to cut through our shields and board us." He pounded the armrest of his command seat. "If I only knew who sabotaged the computer—"

"Minak," Spock said absently. "You gave him access to the Engineering and Computing sections of the ship."

"But how could he have overridden our computer security systems?" Cheyney asked.

"It is difficult but possible to do so," responded Spock,

his fingers rapidly trying another combination. "An isolinear control device would have imitated the computer's normal signal that it was functioning correctly. The dangerous moments would have been connecting and disconnecting the isolinear device. The rest would have been relatively easy. We are fortunate that Minak lacked the time to adapt his altered program into binary language."

"Fortunate!" April's exclamation dripped with sarcasm.

"Yes, because their base four configuration has made them simple to isolate. Now if only—"

"One minute left," Pike said.

"Sir," the communications officer said urgently, "Commander Minak is hailing us."

"Captain April," said Spock almost at the same instant. "I have the code. It is Volash, the name of their jester deity."

"Shall I put him on screen, sir?" asked the communications officer.

April held up his hand. "Just a moment. Spock?"

"I have made the necessary changes," Spock said. "I am restarting all systems . . . now!"

"Shields going to full power!" Lieutenant Belas exclaimed.

"Sir," reported Chief Engineer Powell, "I have damping control. Warp speed available on your command."

"Weapons systems on-line," Belas said.

"Powell, can you reverse the polarity of the tractor beam and channel it dead ahead?"

"Clear out a tunnel among the flies so we can shoot through? Aye, sir!"

"Do it!"

Powell instantly responded. The lights dimmed momentarily. The viewscreen showed the enemy fighters suddenly thrust out of the way ahead of the ship, pushed aside by an invisible, expanding globe of energy. "Give them one warning shot, all laser cannons, dead ahead," ordered April. "Then I want warp four!"

Scarlet beams of energy flashed through the empty space ahead of the *Enterprise*. Then the starfield itself blurred as the great ship leaped from impulse power to faster than light speed. After a second of silence, someone cheered, and then the bridge broke into an excited gabble of congratulations. Already the rebels were light-seconds behind, with no hope of catching up.

April grinned at Spock. "Thank you, young man. You saved our bacon."

Spock lifted an eyebrow. "Animal protein was not involved," he pointed out logically.

Throwing his head back, the captain laughed. "Well, you helped us escape from a bad position then. Son, if you want my recommendation to Starfleet Academy, you've got it."

Spock did not reply. The turbolift doors had opened, and Sarek, clad in his long silvery-gray Vulcan robe, had stepped out. The look he gave his son was grave, tinged with a hint of warning.

Enthusiasm, as Sarek had said, was an emotion and an unseemly one.

Spock wondered if any trace of enthusiasm had shown on his face at the captain's warm words.

Chapter 5

Spock stood in the arched doorway, watching his father. The two of them were back on Vulcan, in the family home. More than two weeks had passed since their escape from the Marathan fighters. In that time, the Federation had come close to sending armed ships against the rebel faction. Only Sarek's considerable powers of persuasion had averted a military reaction.

Now, on his first full day home, Sarek was conferring with the various Marathan parties by subspace communication one at a time, with infinite patience. Spock watched him silently, realizing how hard Sarek's task was. Beyond his father, through one of the many windows, Spock could see the arid, strangely compelling landscape of foothills and rolling plains, with an orange sky overhead. The hot, thin air was a relief after weeks of breathing alien atmosphere, and all in all, being home should have been a welcome experience. And yet . . .

Sarek sat before a subspace viewscreen that filled most of one wall. "I repeat," Spock's father was saying in his soft, even voice, "I cannot understand your people's actions. Starfleet command is most displeased at Minak's attempt on the *Enterprise*. Only the grave importance of Marath as a strategic outpost has prevented the Federation from canceling all exchanges with your people. It required a good deal of insistence on my part to prevent armed retaliation against the rebel fighter fleet."

"I am sorry," said one of the several Marathans on screen. The group of them huddled close together, with one or the other occasionally whispering in the spokesman's ear. All strove to keep their faces blank, betraying no thought, no emotion—a useless endeavor when facing a Vulcan. Far away as he was, Spock recognized signs of tension, repressed anger, deep dissatisfaction. "We of Marath have no control over rebel forces. Surely you understand that."

"I do," Sarek acknowledged. "But, Mr. Ambassador, surely *you* understand that without the cooperation of the Marathans on the planet Shakir, we cannot possibly add the final codicils to the treaty."

"Perhaps you should return," the Marathan suggested.

"No," Sarek said. "An accord imposed from without is no accord at all. It is vital to your people, to your entire star system, to reach agreement. The Shakir delegates have given me no explanation. Ambassador Mar is nowhere to be found, and the others are at odds. They cannot even agree on how to proceed with the treaty." Sarek leaned closer, tenting his fingers. "Sir, I sense some flaw in the treaty—at least from the point of view of the Shakir delegation. What is the significance of Amendment 111?"

"No significance that we need discuss," the ambassador returned quickly. "It merely has to do with certain areas of Marath that the exiles consider an ancient homeland. Of course, our own people live there now. To evict them is impossible. Even if we did so, few of the Shakir colonists would return."

"If we might reconsider the amendment—"

"Even Minak agreed to drop the amendment from consideration," snapped the ambassador. "That should be enough for you."

After a moment of silence, Sarek said, "Let us agree to convene by subspace conference link in three standard days. Perhaps with all parties participating we may be able to resolve this deadlock."

The screen went blank. Sarek leaned back in his chair, and Spock saw how drawn and weary his face looked. Quietly, without speaking to his father, the young Vulcan slipped away.

The day was a fine one, with a warm breeze from the south and the promise of dew later in the evening. Spock found his mother outside, carefully tending her garden. The green expanse was an oasis in the rocky foothills, an exotic one. Amanda Grayson had been a teacher, but she could well have been a botanist. She had a fine sense of what plants would grow or would

not, of how to encourage a vine here, to root an alien shrub there. Her garden represented Vulcan, but more than that, she had planted all sorts of off-world flora. Crimson stalks of Atlantean fire-rod waved in the breeze, close to the intricate blue network of Andorian puzzle-leaf. Pillow-shaped beds of the low-growing *Draebidium froctus* nestled against the crystalline stems of Rigelian lens trees, squat, gnarled miniature trees with crystalline lenses studding their bark. The lenses concentrated sunlight, vastly speeding the trees' photosynthesis and allowing them to spread rapidly—

except that Amanda was trimming them back as Spock watched.

"Hello, Spock," she said without looking up.

"Hello, Mother," Spock returned. "How did you know I was watching you?"

"I've known your step for something like seventeen years," Amanda returned, smiling at him. "It would be strange if I didn't recognize it by now." She finished clipping the lens trees and dropped her shears into a basket. "What do you think?"

Spock said gravely, "The plants appear to respond well to your nurturing. They are healthy and free of parasites."

Amanda laughed. She had tied a scarf around her short hair, and now she unbound it. Spock noted that she was just beginning to show traces of gray.

"Mother," he said, "why did you laugh at me?"

She looked at him with affection. "Oh, Spock, I wasn't laughing *at* you. It's just that you can be so very Vulcan at times."

"But I am Vulcan."

"Only partly," she reminded him. "Let's sit in the shade and enjoy the garden."

A sheltered bench, its roof overgrown with luxuriant goldenweb vines, gave them a cool place to sit. "I want to talk to you," Spock said slowly, "about something that happened on the way home from the Marathan system."

"What you did aboard the *Enterprise* was reported here before you arrived," Amanda told him. "I was in town the day after it happened, and every human I ran into was buzzing with the news that you had saved a Federation ship. They think of you as a hero."

"That is the trouble."

Amanda waited. When Spock did not continue, she said, "Spock, you did a good thing. You used your knowledge to prevent violence. There's nothing wrong with that."

"Perhaps not in itself." Spock took a deep breath. The air in the garden was pleasant, sweet with the flowers that bobbed in the breeze, pungently spicy from some of the alien pollens, an odor like cloves, cinnamon, ginger, and yet unlike them all. "Mother, when the crew thanked me for what I had done, I—I felt gratification."

"Why shouldn't you?"

Spock looked away. Beneath the orange-tinted sky, the hills of Vulcan rolled on to the horizon. "I am a Vulcan," he said simply. "Father has taught me that I must control all emotions rigidly. But of them all, I find the emotions of happiness and pleasure the hardest."

"Because they feel good," Amanda said.

Spock glanced at her face. She had an understanding, kind expression. "Yes," he said simply. "Mother, how does a human cope with such feelings?"

"We give in to them at times," Amanda said. "Spock, do you believe that Vulcans feel no emotions at all?"

Spock considered. "I know that to harbor emotions is destructive to the logical facilities. Therefore, Vulcans have eliminated emotions from their psychology."

"No," Amanda said. "You're wrong."

Surprised, Spock stared at her. "But Vulcans don't feel—"

"Oh, yes, they do," Amanda said. "Spock, you must realize that your father has been very strict with you because you are half human. That is why he has been so insistent that you learn to control your emotions. Did you think you were the only Vulcan who experienced them? You weren't. Don't you remember when you were a child? Some of the other children occasionally mocked you, didn't they?"

"Yes. Because I was different."

"But don't you see? They were giving in to their emotions by doing so. It's just that most Vulcan parents are a little indulgent when their children are very young. They don't begin to teach them the ways of controlling emotion until they're a little older. But Sarek began your training as soon as you could speak and understand. Do you remember falling when you were four years old? We were in the Tascan Mountains, and you slipped down a steep hillside."

Spock shook his head. "I cannot remember."

"You were bruised and scratched when I got to you, but you didn't cry. I asked if you were hurt." Amanda laughed softly. "You replied by giving me a short lecture on the physiological benefits of pain, how it helps an organism to survive by identifying potential threats."

"I still do not remember."

Amanda touched his cheek. "That's all right. The point is that any normal Vulcan child would have cried from pain and fright. At four, you were already too disciplined for that. Spock, have you ever read of the Stoics?"

"A philosophical discipline of ancient Earth?"

"That's Stoicism," corrected Amanda. "The Stoics were the ones who practiced the discipline. They believed that all excessive emotions were bad—too much sorrow, too much joy. They, too, believed in controlling the emotions. But their key was control—they could no more eliminate emotion than you can. Or than your father can."

Spock sighed. "Still, it is disturbing that I felt such sensations when the *Enterprise* crew spoke well of me. They are very different from each other, you know, not like us. I mean—" Spock groped for words, uncharacteristically at a loss. "I mean, all adult Vulcans are alike: serene, humorless, in fundamental agreement. The humans on the *Enterprise* had different backgrounds, different beliefs, different attitudes. They were even competitive. Yet they worked so well together, and each accepted the other."

"Like the IDIC," suggested Amanda gently. "Infinite diversity in infinite combination."

"That applies to the harmony of the universe," Spock said of the Vulcan philosophical principle.

"It can apply to people, too." Amanda rose. "I'm going inside. Think about what we have said, Spock. Talk to me any time about it."

She left him under the shade of the goldenweb. He sat there until the afternoon shadows were long and sharp before, finally, his mind still unclear on certain points, he went inside.

The next morning Sarek dropped the bombshell on him.

Sarek asked Spock to come into his office after breakfast. Sovik, Sarek's assistant and cousin, tactfully left father and son alone. "Well, Spock," Sarek said, "so you were the center of attention on the *Enterprise*. I can understand how difficult that must have been for you."

"Captain April thought the rebels might actually try to kidnap you, Father," Spock said. "I thought there was some urgency in assisting the crew."

"I see." Sarek settled into his chair. "My son, I realize what a strain that must have been. And I could tell that, despite all of your years of discipline, you experienced emotions of pleasure at the crew's reaction to your accomplishment. That was unfortunate."

Spock lowered his gaze. "I did try to control it, Father."

"Of course you did. Well, you are half human after all. A slip like that is not of the gravest importance, although it is regrettable. Still, you must realize that the *Enterprise,* with its undisciplined human crew, is one thing. The Vulcan Science Academy is another."

"I understand."

"Do you? Spock, you must be on your guard at all times. A display of emotion at the Vulcan Science Academy would ruin your chances. It would not be tolerated." Sarek picked up a printed certificate from his desk and looked at it. "That is why I have arranged for you to become a temporary student at the academy for the next four weeks."

Spock tilted his head. "But the next term does not begin until high summer, more than fourteen weeks from now."

"Precisely. I thought that this experience at the academy, before the regular term begins, will allow you to acclimate yourself. To judge how seriously you must take your studies." Sarek passed the certificate to his son. "As you see, the occasion is an intensive four-week seminar on artificial intelligence systems. You will have kinsmen there, and you will meet other Vulcans of your own age. I want you to devote yourself to study—but also pay attention to how other Vulcans behave."

Spock read the certificate. Sarek had certainly worked hard to persuade the administration of the Vulcan Science Academy to admit him: The seminar was for second-year students. "Thank you, Father," he said.

Sarek nodded. "You are welcome. Spock, remember that in our language, the words *science* and *philosophy* spring from the same root. Both disciplines must be pure, logical, and free of emotions. This is your chance to make up for your one slip. Make the best of it."

"I will, Father," Spock said, hoping that Sarek could not detect the doubt that had begun to grow in him like one of Amanda's plants. It might have started as a tiny seed, but the vine had grown strong. Spock felt it inside, like a pressure on his heart, like a pain that warned him of trouble ahead.

Chapter
6

The Vulcan Science Academy, Spock thought, was probably the most rationally designed institution on the entire planet. An intricate complex of gleaming silver and white domes and spires, it had the same logical elegance as a sophisticated exercise in three-dimensional geometry. Symmetry and function, mathematical exactness, and strict logic dictated the curves and sweep of its buildings. Interior rooms all received natural light that saved energy and provided plenty of illumination for their severe, simple functions. Logic dictated the relationship of room to room, building to building. On the outside, walkways and passages never followed twisting, baffling, accidental courses but led naturally, logically, from one place to the next. At the academy, a Vulcan always knew exactly where he stood.

Then, too, the academy blended easily and harmoni-

ously with the tame parkland around it. The carpetlike lawns did not consist of grass, but of a blue-green Vulcan plant that had the same effect. Although they never required mowing, the lawns were even and uniform, perfect squares, rectangles, circles, and trapezoids. The Vulcan trees—some of them actually giant herbs by biological classification—presented flawlessly spherical crowns to the sky. On Earth, such perfection would have come from loving attention and from hours of careful trimming. Here, the trees had been bred for centuries to present a pleasing aspect. Shears never touched them.

Spock walked past a symmetrical group of five trees. Ahead of him, the pathway skirted a circular fountain, a luxury on a naturally arid planet. The water jets took various geometrical forms, cones, parabolas, and hyperbolas. The gentle splashing was almost musical and produced a curiously soothing sensation. By every right, Spock thought, I should accept all this as natural and pleasing. And yet—

And yet.

With a sigh, Spock turned left at the fountain and went into one of the single-story dormitories. Although they were all identical in shape and size, none were named or marked. Similarly, the suites of rooms inside were not numbered. A Vulcan, after all, would note more subtle cues in the slightly varying shades of color, the different orientation of the hallways, that served as well as or better than letters and numbers inelegantly applied to the door.

One such unmarked door sensed and recognized

Spock and opened soundlessly. He stepped into the cool, dark common room of the suite he shared with Sirok, a distant cousin of his. Sirok was nowhere to be seen. Since the door to his private room was closed, Spock deduced that his older cousin was in his own quarters, probably studying or meditating. It was just as well.

Spoke went to his private cubicle. It was severe, plain, undecorated: a simple bed, with no insulating covering (with perfect temperature control, coverlets and blankets were illogical), a desk with its sleek triangular computer pad, and—the one touch of individuality—an elegant, curved Vulcan harp. He touched the strings, producing not music, but rather a soft, cool vibration of sound, a glitter of tones that was at once attractive and a little— though it was an emotional word—sad.

Spoke reclined on the bed and thought about the past few days. Knowing that Sarek had not approved of his reaction to the emergency on the *Enterprise,* Spock had come to the Science Academy fully determined to please his father. He had begun his studies at the academy determined to do everything in accordance with his father's wishes. And yet . . .

And yet his first meeting with his cousin showed him that would not be easy.

"So," his kinsman Sirok had said with the distance and gravity of a twenty-year-old talking to someone two years younger than himself, "I know all about your parentage, Spock. I must tell you that the masters here are most skeptical about your abilities."

Spock had tilted his head and raised an eyebrow. "Indeed?" His voice expressed no distress, only a polite interest. "I do not understand the logic."

"Isn't it plain?" asked Sirok. "Your mother is a human, a member of a notoriously emotional species. The academy demands complete control of one's emotions at all times. Your biological inheritance makes your accomplishing that control problematic. Therefore, since you will have the burden of working extra hard to maintain emotional balance as well as of studying the most rigorous science courses in the galaxy, your teachers are expecting you to fail."

"Ah." After a moment of thought, Spock added, "But permit me to say that I detect a flaw in the reasoning. Although humans feel emotions, even as Vulcans do, it is surely possible that my Vulcan side will allow me to control those feelings without undue stress."

"We regard that as doubtful," Sirok said.

We. Not *they,* but *we.* Sirok considered himself a true Vulcan and Spock, well, something less. That was when Spock first realized that he was alone. True, at the academy several thousand students and instructors surrounded him. Yet of all of them, Spock alone was different, an outsider, an object of curiosity. He wasn't sure that the sensation *disturbed* him, exactly—surely that was too close to a human emotion—but at least he was keenly aware of his difference.

Though, Spock reflected as he lay on his bed, that was no surprise. He had always been something of an outsider, almost an outcast. He had always coped. For a youngster who did not fit in, there was compensations.

He could read, study, take his mind off his solitary state. And now at the Vulcan Science Academy, he had the opportunity of sharing the thoughts of the greatest scientists, even those who had died centuries before and who had left their thoughts behind in written or electronic form. With that kind of company, Spock could hardly call himself lonely.

And yet . . .

That same morning he had participated in a group discussion of recent advances in artificial intelligence technology. Eleven young Vulcans and two elderly ones had gravely, logically, exchanged ideas and observations on submicroscopic circuitry; bicameral, tricameral, and tetracameral logic drivers; and other concerns. The discussion was smooth, rationally perfect, serene. Still, whenever Spock made a comment, he was always aware of a tiny pause before anyone else agreed or took his thought and offered an advancement on it. Perhaps the others did not hold him up to scorn or ridicule, but they *evaluated* him. Without being rude about their doubts, they took a few moments to examine his statements for illogical assumptions, flaws in reasoning, faulty judgment, human emotion.

Perhaps that was really what bothered him the most. At the Vulcan Science Academy, Spock was always under close watch. Everyone—including Sirok—constantly expected him to stumble. They were all waiting, not with glee, but with a kind of patient anticipation. They all seemed so certain of the outcome. He was half human. He would fail.

Rising from his bed, Spock prepared for his afternoon meditation. Instead of considering some scientific proposition or some philosophical question, he reflected on his recent experiences. He chose to concentrate on a comparison of the teamwork aboard the *Enterprise*—a predominantly human affair—with the cooperation he observed at the academy. And he had to admit that in doing so, he discovered a certain disturbing lack of logic.

The next day, after attending a long and intense demonstration of logical programming for robotic subsystems, Spock and Sirok walked out of the cybernetics and robotics building together. "I have an observation," Spock said.

"Really?" Sirok's voice never sounded interested, just cool and a little distant.

"It is this: Today and yesterday I strove very hard to add knowledge to our discussions. I believe that I did so."

"I would agree," said Sirok. "Your observations were accurate and to the point."

Spock took a deep breath. The dry air smelled faintly of water from a distant leaping fountain. "Yet the instructors appear hesitant to acknowledge my contributions. They behave as if what I say lacks validity."

"Of course." Sirok sounded as if it were the most natural behavior in the world.

"Can you explain this?" Spock asked.

Sirok gave him an appraising glance. "I have told you before that everyone here knows of your history and parentage. It is a human failing to arrive at conclusions before thoroughly examining the evidence."

"However," Spock reminded him, "in no case has anyone shown that my conclusions are insufficiently supported."

"No. But there is always the possibility that they will be. Therefore, what you say must be regarded as having less reliability than what I might say or what any other student might say. Of course, your participation in class must be suspect, Spock. A human weakness might show up at any time."

They reached the fountain. "Let us sit here for a few moments," Spock said. They shared a bench facing the astrophysics building's spires and domes. Behind them the water made a rushing, hissing sound as it sprayed in dozens of fan-shaped eruptions. Spock studied the austere buildings as he gathered his thoughts. At last he said, "Sirok, I do not know if you have heard of the passage that my father and I took in returning to Vulcan from Marath."

"I have not."

"We traveled aboard a Starfleet vessel, the *Enterprise*. Do you know of it?"

"Not specifically. I know the general design concepts of Starfleet vessels, of course. Many of their design refinements have come from advances in Vulcan science."

The hot sunlight was almost a physical pressure, heavy on Spock's right cheek and shoulder. A group of three students and one master strolled past, their voices hushed as they discussed a problem in ethics, their shadows dark moving pools beneath their feet. When the four had gone by, Spock said, "Is not the concept of Vulcan science a strange one?"

"How do you mean?"

Spock looked at his cousin. The two were much alike in the Vulcan way: dark hair, pointed ears, sharply slanting eyebrows. Perhaps Sirok was somewhat paler, thinner, taller, and more purely Vulcan. After a moment, Spock said slowly, "I cannot see that there is a Vulcan science and a human science—or any other kind. There is only science."

"That is an illogical statement," Sirok said at once.

"No," Spock insisted. "All science, whether it is Vulcan, human, even Klingon, aims at knowledge and truth. The methods used to gain those goals really do not matter as much as the results do."

"But human science often is stumbling, trial and error, a tedious pursuit," Sirok said. "Vulcan science is thoroughly logical and rational. Because of our methods of thought, our experiments never produce unexpected or unusable results. We are far too disciplined ever to be surprised. Vulcan science is a process of logical unfolding, not of mere discovery." He pronounced *discovery* as though it were a mildly vulgar word.

"I must disagree. Let me give you an example that may show you what I mean. Aboard the *Enterprise,*" Spock said slowly, "I saw a crew of several hundred individuals applying science. They were not a uniform body. Humans are more varied than Vulcans in temperament. And they did not try to conceal their emotions. They

6 3

joked, they became tense, they even were afraid at times. And yet they accomplished their goals. Even more, as they did so, I sensed something there that I do not sense here."

"What is that?"

"Acceptance," Spock said.

Sirok got to his feet. "There. You see exactly your human failing."

Spock squinted up at him. "I am sorry, but I do not."

With a gesture of impatience, Sirok replied, "To desire to be among humans is not logical for a Vulcan. As you yourself just said, humans are slaves to their emotions."

"I do not believe I said that."

"What were your words? 'They did not try to conceal their emotions. They joked, they became tense, they even were afraid at times.' Surroundings like that do not encourage serenity of thought and logical actions. Even worse, such responses are contagious, Spock. If you lived among humans, how long would it be before your heredity made you truly one of them? You have a good mind, my cousin. It would be a shame to make it prey to every disturbing emotion that might come your way."

Spock stood. "My father works with humans and with many other species. Yet I do not believe he has caught the disease of emotion."

"Your father is a Vulcan," Sirok reminded him.

And so the matter rested for another day. Spock kept thinking of arguments he might use to persuade his cousin of his point, and yet he did not use them. For, he thought, what if he is partly correct? *What if the ac-*

ceptance I experienced aboard the Enterprise *has affected me emotionally?* He was not sure that the sensation of belonging, of being accepted for that he was, actually was an emotion. Still, as Sarek had warned him, pleasurable feelings were the most treacherous ones. And certainly he felt the effects of the skepticism that he saw on the faces of his fellow students and—a little better concealed—on those of the Masters.

After the evening meal on the following night, Spock again raised the point with Sirok. They sat in their common room, and their discussion was far too calm to have been called an argument. Spock's words were soft, and Sirok's responses were no louder. Their points were made by logical progression. Still, despite their cordiality, Sirok again was sure that Spock was wrong. "You were raised on Vulcan," he pointed out. "Your father is Vulcan. Therefore, by both education and by heredity, you should be most at home among Vulcans. To think that human associations would be superior is to give in to your weak human heritage—"

A chime interrupted him, three soft chords of music. From Spock's room came a computerized voice: "A message from Sarek for his son, Spock."

Spock rose and hurried into his room. "Spock here," he said to the triangular computer base. "Proceed with your message."

A holographic display, a virtual communication screen, shimmered into existence above his desk. Sarek's face, curiously tense, stared out at Spock. "I have called to tell you to come home at once," Sarek said.

Surprised, Spock glanced at Sirok, who raised one eyebrow in silent inquiry. To his father, Spock said, "Why must I return home, Father?"

"Your mother is recovering," Sarek said.

"What happened?" Spock could not keep an edge of urgency from creeping into his voice, and he spoke more loudly than he had intended.

A flicker of distaste showed in Sarek's eyes. "Spock, do not give in to emotions. I called to tell you that Amanda has been attacked. For your own safety and for that of the family, you must return home at once."

Chapter
7

"Where is Mother?"

Sarek had been deep in conversation with his apprentice T'Lak. At the unexpected interruption, he looked up at his son. "Spock, you have burst in with unseemly haste, and your voice is almost strident."

Spock clenched his hands, fighting for control. T'Lak, a tall young Vulcan woman, glanced down. Although she was a first cousin of Spock's, Vulcans believed that close family exchanges should always be private. Taking a deep breath, Spock murmured, "I apologize, Father. Your communication caused me grave concern. When the pilot of my air car landed on our transportation pad, guards met us. Their presence heightened my concern, and I was carried away."

"The guards are a precaution," Sarek said. "Apparently our family is the victim of some kind of vendetta, a crusade for revenge. It is most illogical, but we must deal with the problem. As to Amanda, she is in her room. You may visit her if you like, but do not upset her. Remember, she is human."

"I am not likely to forget that," Spock said.

He hurried to Amanda's door. The door chimed and announced him, and he heard his mother's voice say, "Come in, Spock."

She lay in bed, covered with an illogical sheet and blanket. Spock's attention focused on the puffy white bandage enclosing his mother's upper left arm. "You were hurt," he said.

"A scratch," Amanda replied. "Come and sit beside me."

Spock took the chair by the bed. His mother's rooms were decorated in Earth fashion, with two-dimensional paintings of landscapes alive with improbable amounts of green, streaked with an exaggeration of water. Her bed, desk, and chairs were all antiques, graceful but not completely suited to function in the logical manner of Vulcan furnishings. "Are you in pain?" Spock asked, feeling awkward and out of place.

"Not anymore. The dressing is an accelerant. I think the wound has closed already, but now the bandage will remove any scar. I'll be fine in three days." She smiled at him. "Thank you for caring."

"It is natural," responded Spock. "I am your son."

"Yes, you are." After a moment, Amanda said, "I suppose you want to know what happened. And I'm sure that Sarek didn't tell you."

"No, he did not. But if you do not wish to speak of it—if the memory is painful—"

"No, I don't mind." Amanda sighed. "It was strange, Spock. Yesterday morning I received a call from town. A man who called himself Wurnall introduced himself as an Arkadian merchant and told me that he had heard I collected exotic plants. He claimed to have a full selection of Ceti IV desert succulents, and he displayed some for me. I bought twenty-five, and he agreed that he would deliver them to me this afternoon. I suppose I should have been suspicious."

"Why is that?"

Amanda shrugged, then made a face. "Ouch. It still gives me a twinge when I move suddenly. Why should I have suspected something was wrong? Well, to begin with, Wurnall didn't really look human. He wore the traditional turban and veil of a Cetan desert nomad, but he was very short and strongly built for a Cetan. And his accent was not quite right—he spoke Vulcan, and so the Universal Translator didn't take over."

Spock nodded. "And the attack?"

"It was a stupid thing. Wurnall arrived late this afternoon, with the plants in two flat cartons. He volunteered to help me carry them into the garden, and I led the way. Just as I was setting my carton down, I heard him drop his, and from the corner of my eye, I saw that he had drawn a weapon, a short, curved dagger. I'm afraid I screamed. Spock, are you all right?"

"Yes, Mother," Spock said.

Amanda gave him an intense look. "You're pale. This is upsetting you."

"I can control my feelings. What happened?"

"Remember I am all right, Spock," Amanda said, touching his hand. "The man slashed at me. I threw up my arms and warded off the attack, but the dagger wounded my left arm. Fortunately, T'Lak was working in the study. She rushed out when she heard my scream. I was backing away from Wurnall and stumbled over the plants—they were rolling everywhere in their little pots. Wurnall was bending over me, ready to strike again, when I saw T'Lak over his shoulder. She simply reached out and gripped his neck, and the man fell unconscious."

"I know the technique," Spock said, "though I have never really used it."

"That's about all," Amanda said. "Except that Sarek is shaken."

Spock's eyes narrowed. "Father? I cannot believe that."

"It's true," Amanda said with a smile. "It is ironic, isn't it? I am the emotional human, but I escaped with nothing more serious than a scratch. Your father is the unemotional Vulcan, but he went into a frenzy of activity, calling you back from the Science Academy, ordering guards from the security service. I think what disturbed him most was discovering that Wurnall was not a Cetan at all, but a Marathan."

Spock gasped. "What?"

"You see? Even you are startled." Amanda yawned. "I am sorry. One effect of accelerated healing is that it makes me very sleepy. Ask your father the rest. And don't worry, Spock. The man is in custody, and I'll be fine." She closed her eyes.

Spock sat beside her bed until he was sure that his mother had fallen asleep. Then he left quietly, careful not to disturb her. He found Sarek in his darkened office, sitting before his computer, his chin resting on his interlaced fingers.

"I am sorry for my behavior earlier," Spock said.

"It was understandable. You may sit if you wish." Spock took a seat beside his father. After a few moments of silence, Sarek said, "Something is terribly wrong. The assassin is a Marathan."

"Mother told me that."

"He is a member of the Minak clan. A former rebel. But he is related to the Tuan clan as well. He will tell the authorities nothing." Sarek sighed. "I have just been in touch with the security director assigned to his case. I am about to go there to urge a mind-meld."

Despite himself, Spock was startled. "Father! A mind-meld is a serious violation of individual privacy."

"I know that very well," Sarek returned. "But I must defend my family, Spock. And even more is at stake. Already some voices are calling for a return to Vulcan's traditional isolation. Our space ports are too open, they say. We have had no serious violence for centuries, but now this happens. All my life I have worked to help Vulcan become a comfortable and valuable part of the United Federation of Planets. It would be a tragic irony if an act directed at my family should result in Vulcan's becoming a closed planet once more."

"I understand," Spock said. "Father, may I accompany you?"

"You are safer here."

In the darkness, Spock could see only the silhouette of his father's face. "I had a Marathan friend," Spock reminded him. "And the trouble affects me personally. And I am your son."

For several seconds, Sarek was silent. Then he pushed himself up from his chair slowly, as if he were an old, tired man. "Very well. Come with me."

The trip to the security center took only a few minutes by air car. Two security officers, a man and a woman, both rather more burly than most Vulcans, led Spock and his father to an extra cubicle, its gray walls plain and empty. At the far end of the room, the captive, a middle-aged Marathan, stood behind a flickering yellowish force field. He wore a plain tunic and trousers, and his face was set in determination, his mouth clamped tightly shut.

"He has said nothing," the woman officer, whose name was T'mar, said quietly.

"That is why I am urging a mind-meld," Sarek returned, glancing at the defiant figure confined behind the force field. "Since we cannot be certain that this is not part of some larger conspiracy, we must take the risk of violating his privacy."

Shanak, the male security officer, shook his head. "No, Sarek. It is impossible."

"But this could be a crisis that affects our people's future relations with every other sentient species," argued Sarek. "Surely the needs of the many outweigh the needs of the one."

T'Mar made a gesture of disagreement. "What you ask might be possible, Sarek, however distasteful, except for one thing."

"And what is the objection?"

T'Mar lowered her voice. "It is a logical objection to which we see no answer. Surely it has occurred to you as well. The treaty of agreement between Marath and the United Federation of Planets is not yet in force."

"Therefore," added Shanak, "Marath is not part of the Federation and is not subject to its laws and regulations. Technically, a mind-meld may be legal if a Federation citizen is apprehended for some crime on Vulcan. But this man is not a citizen."

"Surely," Sarek said, his voice rising just a little, "it is illogical to extend to noncitizens rights and immunities greater than those we offer citizens."

"We do not see it that way," said T'Mar.

The argument went on for many minutes. Spock stopped listening, because he was concentrating on the terrible expression in the captive's eyes. The prisoner's gaze never once left Sarek, and it was venomous, filled with deadly hatred. *This man would gladly kill us all,* Spock thought. *Father, Mother, and me. But why? What strong emotion drives him?*

He stepped away from the group and came closer to the prisoner. Still the Marathan did not look at him, but only at Sarek. Softly, Spock asked, "Why did you attack Amanda?"

The captive gave no sign that he had even heard.

"I must understand," Spock said. "I am Spock, son of Sarek and—"

He flinched back involuntarily. With a howl, the Marathan threw himself at Spock. Unarmed, barefoot, dressed in a thin tunic, apparently helpless, he launched himself with hands clenched like claws. The force field sputtered, buzzed, and hurled him back. He hit the gray wall behind him so hard that the breath chuffed out of his lungs. He slipped to the floor, sprawling, with his back against the wall, and panted.

But his expression did not change, even when T'Mar and Shanak hurried Sarek and Spock from the confinement cubicle. He glared at them with murderous hatred, silent, overpowering, and evil.

The next days were hard ones. Sarek suggested that if Spock wanted to return to the Vulcan Science Academy, he could do so as long as two security officers accompanied him as bodyguards. Spock refused. "That would make me even more out of place than formerly," he pointed out to his father. "I am certain that the presence of security guards would be disruptive. It would be better for me to remain here."

A distracted Sarek agreed. By the next morning, Amanda was out of bed, much better. By the day after that, her physician removed the bandage, and her arm was as good as new. Unfortunately, life in the house was much slower to return to normal.

Sarek tried his best. He installed a complex, sensitive security system, and he made sure that the guards were unobtrusive. Still, he asked Amanda not to go into her garden for a while. "The hills overlook the garden in too many places," he pointed out. "Although it is very unlikely, it is possible that the Marathan may have friends with long-range weapons."

And so the three of them were stuck in the house. They ate together, but Sarek was too wrapped up in the problem of identifying the attacker to be any company. He spent long hours communicating with security headquarters and with the distant representatives of Marath, who denied all knowledge of the assassin's identity.

Spock read, meditated, and became more and more uneasy. He had a sense that something else was about to happen, but what, he could not say. When it came, it caught him by complete surprise.

It came early one morning in the form of a call from Lieutenant Commander Christopher Pike. The young Starfleet officer's smiling face materialized in the virtual screen above Spock's computer. "We meet again," he said. "I hope you are well, Spock."

Realizing that Pike probably had not heard of the assault on his mother, Spock merely nodded. "Thank you, Lieutenant Commander Pike."

"Spock, I'm calling on behalf of Captain April. You might not have thought his compliment was serious, but it was. And he has a considerable amount of influence, so he has an offer for you."

Spock raised his eyebrow. "What kind of offer?"

Pike grinned. "This is the most irregular appointment I ever heard of, but here it is: Captain April proposed you for admission to Starfleet Academy. And you have been accepted."

For a moment, Spock did not reply. He blinked. "I did not request an application."

"I know. Ordinarily, you'd have to take entrance exams, go through the selection process, et cetera, et cetera, et cetera. But you have unusual qualifications. You have already been accepted to the Vulcan Science Academy, whose standards are at least as high as Starfleet's. And then, too, you helped us get the *Enterprise* out of a tough spot." Pike's expression became more serious. "Spock, we humans are grateful for Vulcans joining Earth as a founding member of the Federation. And we appreciate Vulcan's contribution of the *Intrepid* as a Starfleet vessel—you probably know that the entire crew of the *Intrepid* is made up of Vulcan Science Academy graduates. But there's a general feeling in Starfleet that *all* of our starships would benefit from having Vulcan officers. You can open the door for them. You can be the first Vulcan cadet at Starfleet Academy."

"I do not know what to say," Spock confessed.

"Think it over," advised Pike. "I know you'd be a fine officer. And surely joining Starfleet would be a logical step for someone of your background. We'll need an answer in three standard months. I hope you'll decide to accept."

"You are fond of your career in Starfleet," Spock said.

"I wouldn't be happy doing anything else," Pike returned.

When Pike broke the communications link, Spock stared into space. His friend in Starfleet did not know it, but his offer had complicated Spock's life. If Spock were fully human, the invitation would have made him deliriously happy. But Spock was half Vulcan.

It only made him more confused and uncertain than ever.

Chapter
8

Sarek's expectation of another attack was accurate. The news came the next morning—from the Vulcan Science Academy. Sarek called Spock in, and the two of them heard the grim report from a security officer on the viewscreen. "Sirok was seriously wounded," the officer said. "He is in the Healing Center now. He will recover, but the process will be a long one. He suffered internal trauma."

"Sirok?" Spock asked. "When did this happen?"

The security officer said, "Not more than an hour ago. The event was captured by security sensors. Would you care to see?"

"Yes," Sarek said.

"Very well." The officer touched a control panel before him. The picture changed, showing a walkway beside one of the fountains on the academy grounds. Two young Vulcans passed, going in opposite directions. The

guard's voice said, "Sirok was on his way to a seminar. He will be visible in three seconds."

And three seconds later, the tall, robed figure of Sirok appeared. The young Vulcan was walking slowly, his head down, his palms pressed together before him, as he often did when pondering some question of science. "I will slow the action," the security officer said.

From the lower corner of the screen, a short, burly figure rushed into view, moving fast even in slow motion. Spock tilted his head. He saw the figure's arm sweep up. "Please stop the action," Spock said.

The picture froze. Sirok was just beginning to react. The assassin had gripped the edge of his robe with one hand, and the other held a curved blade high overhead. Spock leaned closer to the display. "Magnify the weapon five times please."

The weapon, immobilized on the screen, became larger. It was of some silvery-gray substance, not metal. And blade and handle were not two separate pieces, but one continuous carved surface. "Father," Spock said, "notice the Marathan glyphs on the blade."

"I see them, Spock," Sarek returned. "They are the Lorval clan symbols—the same as those on the blade that wounded your mother." Sarek spoke a little more loudly: "Thank you. Please restore the image and resume slow motion."

They saw the blade plunge downward. Sirok reached out, fingers curved, trying for a neck pinch, but his assailant had taken him by surprise. His face contorted as the blade, hidden from view by the assassin's body, found its mark. He reeled backward, striking the curving base of the fountain. Sirok fell to the ground and rolled, leaving a spatter of copper-green blood. The assassin leaped toward him, but at that moment, two Vulcans ran into the picture. The attacker spun, brandishing his dagger, his iridescent hair flying with the motion. He yelled something, and then a sonic beam struck him, sending him crumpling to the ground.

"He was stunned, of course," the security officer said. "He is in custody, but he refuses to answer our questions."

"What did he cry out just before falling unconscious?" asked Sarek.

"That is why we called you." The security officer appeared on the screen once more. "He thought his victim was dead. Apparently the assassin was unfamiliar with Vulcan anatomy and was under the impression that he had struck Sirok in the heart. He shouted, 'Sarek's son is dead—next is Sarek.' "

Sarek blinked. "My son?"

"He must have waited outside the residence building. Sirok and your son, Spock, are somewhat similar in appearance. The assassin believed he was striking at Spock."

"Why me?" asked Spock. "That is illogical. I have done nothing to warrant an attack."

"Nor has your mother," the officer reminded him. "And alien species do not often behave logically."

Sarek straightened. "Keep me informed of anything the prisoner says. I am trying to persuade the authorities to permit a mind-meld."

"If you will forgive my saying so, Sarek, that will be difficult. But we will do as you request."

The virtual screen vanished. Sarek looked at his son. "Why?" he asked. When Spock raised an eyebrow, Sarek shook his head. "A rhetorical question only. Of course, you do not know why. It is a disturbing development. If the different parties to the Marathan treaty indeed were in disagreement, why did they pretend to agree at Bel T'aan?"

"I do not know," Spock said. He frowned slightly.

"But perhaps the attacks really are not a direct result of the treaty. It is possible that the rebel factions who attempted to immobilize the *Enterprise* lost face when I found a way for the ship to escape. I do know that Marathan fighters have a fierce pride. Perhaps the vendetta is a punishment for a perceived humiliation."

Sarek considered that, but his expression showed that he did not accept the possibility. "No, Spock. The trouble must have begun earlier, with the treaty. I must review every clause in it carefully to see what objection the rebel forces may have. And the treaty will give us our best chance of finding the other assassins."

"You believe there are more?"

"Certainly there are more," Sarek replied. "The authorities have told me that a number of Marathans are presently on Vulcan. Those who can be accounted for appear to be peaceful traders, all from the home planet. But some have simply disappeared. Their refusal to obey Vulcan law is a major reason for the debate currently going on about sealing Vulcan from the galaxy. It is a trivial problem, really, since it focuses on our family only—"

"It is not trivial to us," Spock objected.

"The needs of the many, Spock," Sarek reminded him. "At any rate, if I let it be known that I plan to transmit the treaty to Federation headquarters for final ratification, I believe the assassins will make a concerted effort to stop me."

"You mean to kill you."

"Yes."

Spock stared at his father. "But would you lie, Father?"

"No. I will merely let everyone know that it is my intention to transmit the treaty, as it really is—eventually. I will put no date on the transmission, however, and I will arrange to travel to Earth in person. Any spies will assume that the purpose of my trip is to ratify the treaty. That should bring the remaining assassins into the open."

"It is dangerous," Spock said.

"I have weighed the danger."

Spock paced, his head down. "Father, allow me to study the treaty with you before you take this step. Perhaps together we can discover the problem."

"I would be gratified by your help, my son. The language of diplomacy is an important acquisition, even for one who wishes to be a scientist."

They worked in the confinement of their home. Sarek even darkened the windows, allowing no chance for an outsider to peer into the house from a distance. Spock noted the methodical, logical structure of the treaty. Under even the closest analysis, the agreement seemed fair to all sides. The treaty specified that each party, homeworlders and colonists, would have absolute control of their own territory. However, Marathans also gained freedom of movement within the system as long as visitors agreed to abide by the rules and laws of local governments. And the spaceways remained open to all.

Despite his wish to discover a weak point, Spock had to admit that his father had done an excellent, flawless job. To a Vulcan, at least, the treaty had not even the tiniest imperfection.

That did not keep Spock from trying over and over. Late at night, when Sarek and Amanda were asleep, Spock sat at his computer, studying each paragraph, each sentence, each word of the treaty. He reviewed Marathan history to no avail. And he realized that if his study did not pay off, soon his father would make himself a highly visible target for the assassins.

The day came when both father and son had to admit defeat. "Well," Sarek said, "there is one hope left."

"Sarek, no." Amanda stood in the doorway, her face a mask of worry. "I don't want you to be a—a decoy. It's too dangerous."

Sarek went to his wife and took both of her hands in his. "Events are at a crisis," he told her gently. "Those who oppose Vulcan's membership in the Federation have strong voices. I cannot allow them to use this incident as an excuse to ruin everything that I have worked for. To do so would be worse than dying."

"I'll go to Earth with you," Amanda said.

Spock felt a curious hollow sensation inside. Fleetingly he wondered what would happen if Sarek agreed—and somehow the assassins succeeded. Both of his parents could be killed. But Sarek said, "No. That would not be logical. You have never accompanied me on a diplomatic mission before, and surely any observer would know that."

"Mother has not accompanied you," said Spock. "But I have."

They both looked at him. "It is logical," Spock said. "I was with you when you negotiated the treaty. Why should I not be with you when you take it to Earth?"

"No," Sarek said. "It is far too dangerous."

"For me, but not for you?"

"Spock," Amanda said, crossing to him, "I don't want you to go either."

"I know, Mother. But you would go."

"I belong with Sarek."

"As do I," Spock reminded her. "Father, you must admit that two of us would be more likely to withstand an attack than one. Surely that is logical."

Sarek nodded. "But you wish to be a scientist, not a diplomat. It is *not* logical for a young scientist to go on a diplomatic mission."

"It is," Spock said simply, "if the Marathans do not know that I wish to be a scientist and not a diplomat."

The argument—if anyone could call the reasonable, soft exchange between father and son an argument—went on for a long time. At last they reached a compromise.

"Very well," Sarek said. "I will announce my departure for Earth as coming in one week. Today I must travel into town to speak to the regional justice committee. They have pointed out that we are still holding two unidentified Marathans and have not yet set a date of trial for them. This is my last chance to obtain permission for a mind-meld, and failing that, I must at least arrange for a trial. You may come with me on this trip if we take all precautions."

Spock nodded his agreement. "And if I prove to be of assistance this time, then you will consider allowing me to accompany you to Earth."

"My son," Sarek said in his dry way, "I advise you to reconsider your choice of careers. You would make a fine diplomat after all."

Sarek took no chances. The security guards did a full area scan before he and Spock emerged from the house. For a moment, Spock blinked in the torrid, bright sunlight. Days inside the house made the brilliant day almost painful. The far horizon shimmered with heat waves, and the air car's external alloy skin was sizzling hot. As soon as they were aboard, Sarek raised shields—not a usual option on air cars, but this one had been specially equipped. Spock sat beside his father as the car rose, swiveled, and accelerated above the dry plain below.

They followed the deep gorge of a river for part of the way. Looking down, Spock saw leaping herds of *quattils,* herbivorous creatures native to Vulcan. Once, ages ago, *quattils* had been the prey of flying creatures. These predators had become extinct, but still the *quattils* fled whenever the shadow of an air car passed over them, driven by a deep and ancient instinct.

Spock reflected on that. Perhaps, he thought, in some ways the Marathans were acting on a hidden instinct. Something that lay deep under the surface of their minds. But what could it be?

The throaty hum of the air car engine, the vibration, lulled him. He had missed a great deal of sleep in the past few days. He almost nodded off. They came to the outskirts of the city, its buildings low and cool, ancient stone and alloy buildings lining the perfectly squared streets. Sarek dropped to street level and cruised the air car slowly along. "Why have you descended?" asked Spock. "We could easily have landed on the secure deck at the House of Justice."

"I wish our presence to be obvious," Sarek returned.

They passed the space port. Spock looked out the window at the crowds: Humans, almost panting in the thin, hot air, walked side by side with blue-skinned Andorians, their antennae drooping and their steps slow in the gravity of Vulcan. A group of short, muscular Tellarites strode along with more assurance, though bearded and furred as they were, they must have suffered from the heat. The streets around the entry port were an untidy assortment of Vulcan and off-world shops and stores. Vulcans disliked anything untidy. Perhaps this was one reason, Spock thought, that so many powerful Vulcan leaders were campaigning to close the ports, eject the aliens—

He sat up, turning his head sharply. He thought—

"What is it, Spock?"

Spock forced himself to settle back. "Nothing, Father. I thought I saw someone that I last met aboard the *Enterprise*."

"Hardly likely. That ship is far from here by now."

"I was possibly mistaken."

They did not speak again, and although they reached the House of Justice at ground level, Sarek powered the air car for a hop up to the secure landing site. They passed through a force field meant to shield them against any high-speed energy weapons, and Sarek set the car down gently within a few meters of the portal. He and his son hurried inside.

In the cool darkness of the House of Justice, Spock patiently listened to his father's arguments. He knew they would be disregarded. The ancient Vulcan teacher Surak, he who had at last brought an end to war on Vulcan, had taught the sanctity of the individual. Except by mutual consent, Vulcans almost never mind-melded. Rare exceptions were made only for Vulcans suffering from mental illness. And although, under their agreement with the Federation, Vulcans theoretically could use the mind-meld to read the thoughts of an alien species, that had never been done. The Justices, three elderly women, were not eager to create a precedent.

When they rejected Sarek's request, Sarek smoothly turned to the question of trial. Vulcan trials were scrupulously fair, even when the accused chose to mount no defense. The Justices did agree to appoint a day for the two captives to be tried, and that was that.

Sarek chose to fly home at a higher altitude, and so Spock did not have another chance to look at the crowds in the streets.

Still, he thought he had what he needed. The figure he had seen looked a great deal like a Tellarite. Hooded, squat, its face obscured by a heavy beard, the person would never be mistaken for a Vulcan. The disguise was a logical one.

But Spock had seen through it. In the way it moved, in its startled reaction to a glimpse of Spock's face, the disguised figure had given itself away. It was no Tellarite.

It was undoubtedly Cha-Tuan Mar Lorval—Spock's friend.

Or was he now Spock's assassin?

Chapter 9

Night, thick and dark outside. The house was quiet, with no hint that wakeful guards waited at strategic points beyond the walls and manned a security station inside. Spock, alone in his room, finished the last adjustment. "Computer," he said.

"Working," responded a soft, disembodied voice.

"I have integrated a Series 15,000 Artificial Intelligence Module with your operating unit. It is an experimental design, but I believe it will augment your operation. Please test all functions."

For the space of a heartbeat the computer was silent. Then it reported, "All functions are normal."

Spock leaned back. "Very well. I need to access the security visuals grid on the south side of Space Port Prime. Take steps to conceal the link from anyone who might be monitoring the security system."

The machine had no sense of legality or illegality, and it did not question the order. "Working. Visuals grid is available. The link is secure."

"Give me a visual display beginning ..." Spock thought and then gave a precise time estimate: that afternoon when he and his father had passed the space port.

"Working." The display flickered into existence. Spock studied the still picture.

"Advance in standard seconds," he said.

The display changed, a series of still pictures. All were from one vantage point, and since they flicked into and out of existence at the rate of one per second, Spock saw a kind of jerky motion picture of the street, with people hitching along. "Stop," he ordered after only seven seconds. The air car that he and his father had used was visible, nosing into the picture from the right side. Spock scanned the crowd. "Advance in standard seconds, but hold each view for five seconds," he ordered.

The air car moved to the center of the field, then off the left edge of the picture. "Next vantage point." The field of view shifted northward. Now the car was in the right corner again, but a different section of the street appeared. "Stop. Overlay a coordinate grid."

A yellow network of lines appeared over the picture. Spock isolated the figure he had seen. "Enlarge sections Alpha 3 to Alpha 6, Beta 3 to Beta 6, Gamma 3 to Gamma 6."

The squares enlarged to fill the whole screen. "Delete grid." Spock leaned back. He was looking at Cha—and

Cha seemed to be looking at him. In his hood and mask, he would pass for a young Tellarite male, but his eyes were unmistakable. "Computer," Spock said. "Isolate this subject in your memory. Access security networks as necessary. Follow the movements of this subject and let me know where he is at this moment."

"Working."

"Display a map of his movements."

A glowing map of the city appeared, with the route of Spock's target marked in a fluorescent green line. Cha had reversed his direction a moment after spotting Spock and his father. He had taken a winding path across the city as if unfamiliar with its streets—or as if trying to throw off any trackers. The line came to rest in a block of buildings equipped with special environmental controls for atmosphere and gravity, the domiciles of alien traders and visitors who liked some variation from the Vulcan conditions.

Spock laced his fingers together and brooded. He could tell his father, or he could alert the security forces. Or . . .

Taking a deep breath, Spock weighed the alternatives. What if Cha were not a willing visitor to Vulcan? Could he be a hostage, perhaps, and disguised in an attempt to escape from the militant faction of Marathans? Or was he here as a spy? Or perhaps had he come to warn Spock?

"Computer," Spock said, "display the original picture of the target."

And there was Cha again, his eyes staring out of the

Tellarite mask. "Computer, interpret the emotions of the target."

"Unable to complete the task," the computer responded. "Do you need more data?"

"Affirmative," said the artificial voice. "Please give a complete working definition of the term *emotions.*"

"Cancel the order."

"Canceled."

The night was well advanced. Spock had to make up his mind, and yet how could he? Who knew what a Marathan's emotions were like? Spock only remembered that Cha, like himself, had felt like an outcast.

The young Vulcan lowered his head for a moment, then spoke with decision: "Computer, I give you this task. Currently this house is under surveillance of an advanced security and detection system. Find a way for me to disable the system just long enough to get away from the house undetected."

"Working."

"Estimate of time required for the task."

"Three hours, thirty-nine minutes, eleven point fifty-five seconds, standard."

"Wake me when you have completed the task."

"Affirmative."

Utterly weary, Spock leaned back in his chair. He closed his eyes, cleared his mind, and in less than a minute, he was asleep. Such relaxation called for the careful discipline of a Vulcan mind—or for the absolute exhaustion of a human one.

*   *   *

Spock woke to the gentle jingling of a chime. "The problem is solved," the computer said. "Time elapsed: three hours, thirty-seven minutes, three point zero one seconds, standard."

"Less than your estimate. Very efficient."

"Yes. I will cause a minor malfunction that will engage the attention of the guard on the northwest side of the property. While he is attending to the problem, you may leave the environment at any time within the next two minutes, moving quietly. As soon as you are outside the detection field, I will reactivate the security system. The security monitors will be altered to give a false reading indicating that you are safely asleep in your bed."

"Very good." Spock rose, instantly alert, and hurried outside, taking with him only a portable communicator. From the front, he could see the guard bent over a hand-held read-out device, trying to adjust the controls. On silent feet, Spock hastened away from the house, descending the flank of a bare, rocky hill. Dawn was approaching fast, and already the eastern sky showed a tinge of red. Spock hurried without quite running until he was four kilometers or so away from the house. Then, using his communicator, he summoned an air car from the public transportation authority in the city. A few minutes later, the vehicle hummed into sight, flying on autopilot. It landed on a flat, sandy expanse, the floor of a long-dried lake, and Spock climbed into the pilot's seat, hoping he was not about to make the worst mistake of his life.

By the time he reached the outskirts of the city, the

sun was up, throwing long, sharp shadows over plain, market squares, and streets. Spock landed the air car on a public transportation pad, indicated on its control panel that he would not need the vehicle again, and walked several blocks. The low sun sent its rays hot and almost horizontal along the side streets. In between the intersections, the shadows were still crisp and dark. When Spoke came to a halt, he stood in an archway that looked out toward the block of alien domiciles his computer had isolated. The morning chill was dissolving under the fierce rays of the sun. He hoped that Amanda and Sarek would decide to let their son sleep. He needed as much time as he could steal to carry out his plan. Spock settled into the shadows and waited.

But not for very long. Within the hour, a stocky figure emerged, looked both ways, and then blended in with the early-morning pedestrians. Spock followed the hooded, robed individual, gradually coming closer. When they cut through a section of the city given over to a green park, its walls breaking it up into mazelike squares, Spock hurried ahead, coming almost close enough to tap his quarry on the shoulder. "Cha!" he said loudly.

The figure six steps ahead of him bolted and ran, cutting to the left and crossing a street. Spock ran after him. Vulcan heads turned sharply—Vulcan boys of Spock's age no longer played, and it was unseemly to run. Spock ignored them, his eyes locked on the hooded, cloaked figure ahead of him. A zig, a zag, and Spock's prey made a serious mistake, diving into a narrow alley between two blank-walled stoned buildings. Spock reached a point where the alley bent at a right angle and saw that Cha was at a standstill, his back to the wall. "Cha," he said, "we must talk."

The Tellarite vanished. Cha stripped off the hooded cloak, the lifelike prosthetic mask, and stood revealed as himself. "We have nothing to talk about, Vulcan!"

"On the contrary," Spock said, stepping forward. "I think that the two of us may be able to avoid—"

Cha roared out, an inarticulate bellow, and dived forward, reaching for Spock. Fast as he was, Spock was too slow to react. Cha's strong arms gripped him, and the two fell to the ground, Cha raging as he tried to pin the Vulcan. He fumbled at his belt, at a curved scabbard. Spock gripped the Marathan boy's wrist, desperately trying to keep him from drawing his weapon.

Spock was on his back. He bent his knees and got his feet into the pit of Cha's stomach. Rolling, Spock kicked at the same time, flipping Cha heels over head. The Marathan landed on his back with a gasp, but immediately he scrambled up again. Spock crouched, facing him. Cha's eyes were wild, furious. "Cha," Spock said, "I must ask you—"

No good. Cha charged again, but this time Spock was ready. He seized Cha's shoulder at the base of the neck, spread his fingers, and manipulated the nerve junctions that virtually all humanoid species had at those points. He felt Cha stiffen, then collapse. Spock caught him, eased him to the ground. He looked behind him. No one was in the alley, and from here, they could not be seen from the street. He waited.

After a few minutes, Cha groaned. He sat up suddenly, reaching for his belt.

"I have removed your weapon," Spock said. He held up the carved curved Marathan dagger.

Cha backed away, sat with his spine against the blank stone wall. "Well, use it then," he growled. "Kill me."

"I have no desire to do that. To injure you would be illogical."

Amber-colored tears brimmed in Cha's eyes. "You have humiliated me," he said in a gruff voice. "It will be a disgrace to my family if you do not kill me."

"Killing is not the Vulcan way," Spock replied. "You can trust me."

When Cha did not respond, Spock gravely offered him the dagger, grip end first. Cha darted a look of wild suspicion at the young Vulcan. "What kind of trick are you playing?"

"No trick," Spock said. "I did not mean to humiliate you. Here is your weapon. I hope you will not use it."

Cha took it from Spock, stared at the curved blade, ran his finger over the Marathan glyphs. Then he replaced the weapon in the scabbard. "Go."

"Not yet," Spock insisted. "Cha, permit me to say that the warfare in the Marathan system has been illogical. Over the centuries, many thousands of your people have died in battle, and many millions have died indirectly from warfare. It is illogical for a species to destroy itself. Now the treaty has offered your people a way out of their hostility and hatred. Why has your clan and that of the rebels turned against it?"

"I cannot speak of such things!" Cha's face wore a baffled expression. "You can't possibly understand. Some things are not permitted—"

"The same is true here," Spock pointed out. "By finding you, I have violated my father's wishes. Yet I have the hope that finding you can produce a greater good."

For a moment, Cha seemed on the verge of some confession, but then he half-turned and stared at the ground. "A Marathan man may not speak of certain things," he muttered. "It is forbidden."

Silence. From the hidden mouth of the alley, murmuring voices as small groups of people walked past, unaware of the two young men around the corner. The sky overhead was a sullen orange red, the shadows in the alley deep and purple. Spock said slowly, "May I point out, Cha, that neither of us is technically a man? Back on Marath, on the last night at Bel T'aan, you told me the story of Volash and Hamarka. You said you were not yet of age, and so you could tell me that."

"That is not True Lore," Cha maintained stubbornly. "The secrets of our belief—those I can never reveal to an outsider."

"You are an outsider."

Cha flashed him an angry glare. "All of my clan are outsiders!" he snapped. "Thrown off our world by those who disagreed with our beliefs, our customs. You don't know what it's like."

Spock put a hand on Cha's shoulder. "You are mistaken," he said simply. "I know very well what it is to be an outsider."

Cha wrenched his shoulder away, as if Spock's touch were painful. "You can't."

"But I do. The two of us, Cha, do not belong. And yet we need to belong. I suggest that you could do your people more good than you know by sharing with me the secret cause of your clan's vendetta against my father."

"Your father betrayed us!"

Spock shook his head. "That would not be my father's way. You do not know him, but I do. Cha, once on Marath you trusted me. Trust me again. If there is anything that my father can do to set things right, he will try. You have my word on it."

For a moment, Cha stared into Spock's eyes, uncertainty flickering in his expression. He licked his lips. "Spock," he said hoarsely, "there is a homing device in my blade. I activated it when you returned it to me. For your own safety, leave now."

"No."

"You don't understand! My people are sworn to kill you—"

"Then you will have to persuade them not to kill me."

Cha glanced anxiously toward the angle of the alley. "I am not yet a man," he muttered. "I have not yet undergone the Ceremony of Bonding. Perhaps—but it is True Lore you ask me to speak of!"

"I will never reveal it without your permission," Spock said.

"If I tell you, will you go?"

1996

Spock nodded.

Cha leaned close and whispered. Spock tilted his head, listening as if he were a confessor listening to a repentant criminal's plea for forgiveness. A momentary expression of surprise flashed across his face and one of understanding. "I see," he said at last. "But, Cha, you have been misled. The one who must be behind this is not my father, but—"

"Cha!" The harsh voice whirled them both around. Karos Mar Santor, wearing no disguise apart from a brown hooded cloak, stood behind them. He raised a stubby weapon, a device like a silvery test tube, closed and rounded at both ends.

"No, Father!"

Spock saw circles of energy leap from the end of the weapon, bluish expanding ripples in the air rushing toward him. He opened his mouth to speak, but the disruptor beam took him in the chest. Spock felt himself slammed backward. Everything happened too slowly, like actions in a nightmare. The toppling Spock stared straight up at the orange-red sky, then saw it darken and recede. He felt himself falling backward, down into a dark, bottomless pit. He struggled to breathe, but his lungs would not work. Everything around him, colors, sounds, faded. Spock wondered when he would stop falling.

He passed out before discovering if he ever would.

Chapter
10

An eternity of drifting in a gray void, struggling against nothing. *Is this death?* Spock wondered, almost too empty to care. But something told him it was not, and something made him struggle, like a swimmer far below the surface desperately trying to rise again and gulp life-giving air.

Then something, a blurry light place in the thick, dark fog, and a voice from somewhere faraway, speaking his name. He tried to answer and found he could not. *Towkath.* The Vulcan term floated into his mind. It described a trance state. Badly injured Vulcans could enter *Towkath,* go dormant, allow their body's defenses to repair damage at peak efficiency. It was a learned skill, not an instinct, but Spock had learned it. Now he fought to break the trance, paying for his attempt with sudden, wrenching pain.

He groaned, and he must have made a sound, for the blurred face was back, hovering over him in the grayness. "Spock?"

"Fa—father," croaked Spock. He forced his eyes to focus. Sarek, yes, and Amanda beside him, both leaning over Spock. The young Vulcan realized with a shock that he was at home, his own room.

"Oh, Spock," Amanda said, her eyes wild with worry.

Sarek placed a hand on his shoulder. "You were attacked by a Marathan wielding a neural disruptor weapon," his father said. "Fortunately, the security sensors picked up the discharge of energy, and the authorities captured the two assassins before they could fatally injure you. They—"

"Codicil," groaned Spock.

Sarek frowned. "What?"

"Father, you must add a codicil to the Marathan treaty." Spock raised up in bed, gripping is father's arm with terrible urgency. Sarek, with a flash of distaste, pulled back, away from the emotional display. Spock spoke in a tumble of words: "You were betrayed on Marath by Hul Minak Lasvor. He was to tell you of the importance of certain ancient religious sites on the planet. He did not because he wished the civil war to continue. He has dreams of conquering Marath from space, of restoring his clan to the leadership of the entire system."

"Calm yourself, Spock." Sarek's voice had a faint, displeased note, a stern tone that he almost never used. "I do not understand what you are saying."

Spock sat on the edge of his bed, his head spinning. He closed his eyes and forced himself to speak slowly, rationally. "Father, the Marathans have strong, ancient religious taboos. On the planet there is a high plateau called P'ik ban Aldor. It is a shrine, the center of all Marathan religions."

"I have never heard that."

"Because of the religious taboos," insisted Spock. "The Marathans may not mention their beliefs to outsiders. But their priests did delegate one man, Hul Minak Lasvor, to communicate their desires and demands to you. He did not, and so in the treaty you did not mention complete and free access to P'ik Ban Aldor for all Marathans."

Sarek sank into a chair beside Spock's bed. "I see. And his motive was to prolong the war?"

Spock nodded. "He blamed you. The off-world colonists could not refuse to sign the treaty that they had negotiated, or they would lose face. But once away from the planet, Minak convinced the others that the planet-dwelling Marathans had bribed you to omit guarantees of religious tolerance. The opening of P'ik Ban Aldor for all believers was to have been the symbol for that tolerance."

Sarek rose. "I will question the captives," he said.

"Father!" Spock's weak croak stopped Sarek in the doorway. "Cha and his father—were they taken?"

"They are captured and the other members of their clan as well. None of them were seriously injured."

"Do not let them know where you learned this," said Spock. "Otherwise Cha will become an outcast."

Sarek nodded, and as he turned, Spock sank back on the bed. "I am very tired," he said.

He felt Amanda's hand, cool and soft, on his forehead, and he drifted to sleep again.

A time of healing and slowly returning strength followed. A dazed Spock woke only long enough to take a little nourishment, and then he sank back into the depths of *Tow-kath,* the healing fever. Drifting dreams disturbed him. He saw himself on the *Enterprise,* grimly trying to avoid some kind of catastrophe but failing because he could not move fast enough. He was on the grounds of the Vulcan Science Academy, witnessing an attack on Sirok, but when he tried to run to his cousin's aid, the pathway turned to mud and made him stagger forward in nightmare sluggishness. He saw himself speaking to a group of students at the academy, with all of them murmuring, "Not logical. You are not logical."

But finally a day came when he opened his eyes, searched for the pain, and found it had vanished. He rose and dressed, and he met Amanda in the doorway. "You are better," she said, and impulsively she embraced her son.

"How long has it been?" he asked.

She led him to her room, made him sit in a chair. "You have been asleep, more or less, for a week. So much has happened."

"Sirok. I dreamed of him."

"Sirok is well. He has recovered, and he will be back at the Vulcan Science Academy within a month." Amanda shook her head as she studied her son's face. "A neural disruptor set to kill is a terrible weapon," she said softly. "It destroys major nerve junctions, and they cannot be restored. You were very close to death."

"I know. The security officers saved me."

Amanda smiled. "No," she said softly. "Your friend saved you."

Spock raised an eyebrow. "I do not understand."

"Cha," said Amanda. "He threw himself in front of the disruptor beam. His father dropped the weapon, certain that he had killed his son. Marathans are even more susceptible to disruptor effects than Vulcans."

"Their neurons are not as well shielded as ours," Spock said.

Amanda almost laughed. "For *whatever* reason. When the security officers arrived, Karos Mar Santor was holding his son's body. The nerves of his lower spine were badly hurt by the disruptor. He could not move his legs, and he was in pain. They took Cha to the House of Healing, and fortunately the damage was not permanent. He will walk with a limp for a long time, but he'll recover full use of his legs eventually."

"I see. The treaty?"

"Sarek is planning to return to Marath in six weeks, as soon as Cha is well enough to travel. Santor's people—"

"Mar's people," Spock corrected. "The Marathan family name comes second."

"Very well," Amanda said. "Mar's people have taken

Hul Minak Lasvor into custody. They will try him according to their laws. Sarek believes that he can negotiate a treaty that will allow all sides free access to some site on the planet that seems very important to them."

"I am sure he will succeed."

"Aren't you happy for him then?" asked Amanda.

"Mother!"

Amanda chuckled. "At least you show *some* emotion. I believe I shocked you that time!"

Spock considered. "I was not shocked. I was surprised at how illogical you can be."

Days later, Spock stood beside Cha, who had walked a little for the first time since his father had tried to kill Spock. Cha, thinner, exhausted, sat in a hover chair in the solarium of the House of Healing. Through a huge curved window he looked out across the city, toward the west. The dry landscape of Vulcan rolled away to the horizon. Hot afternoon sunlight poured in. "Your world is like Marath in some respects, but it is very different, too. Not as much water, different colors, a strange sky. And yet it has beauty of its own," Cha said.

"I wanted to thank you," Spock said softly. "You saved my life."

Cha twisted away awkwardly, not letting Spock see his face. When he spoke, his voice was gruff, full of feeling: "Friends do that."

"Yes," Spock said, considering. "I suppose they do."

For some minutes the two sat together without speaking. Then Cha cleared his throat. "I will celebrate my

birthday on the way back home, Spock. As soon as we arrive at Shakir, my father and my uncles will join me to perform the Ceremony of Bonding. Then I will be a man." He glanced at Spock. "Everything in my life will change from then on. No more childish disobedience. No more sharing secrets with alien friends."

"That will be a loss," Spock said. "But in accepting adulthood, you will gain much as well."

"I hope to be a leader of my people in time," Cha said. "You Vulcans have much to teach Marathans. We are a violent and illogical people. Perhaps we can learn from you to control our hurtful emotions. To get along with each other. I wish I could help all Marathans learn that lesson." With a grin, Cha said, "It would be wonderful if I became the chief counselor of the Marathans and you the ambassador from Vulcan."

This time Spock looked away. "Only time will show if that is possible."

"Thank you, Spock."

"On the contrary. Thank you, Cha."

Weeks passed. Cha and his family, Sarek and his aides, left Vulcan for Marath. Before long, Sarek called home to tell Amanda and Spock that the treaty had been successfully amended. "Working out the language was very difficult, because we had to refer to things that cannot be named, but somehow we have succeeded. Now all sides can at last agree," Sarek said. "And Marath will become a member of the Federation."

"And Vulcan?" Spock asked. "Has the crisis passed here, too?"

Sarek nodded. "An acute question. Things have changed because this problem has been successfully resolved despite the warnings of those who fear outsiders. The power of the opposition party has waned. Vulcan will not close itself off from other worlds. More logical minds have prevailed."

"That is good."

"I think so. I must prepare for the return voyage now. Amanda and Spock, live long and prosper."

Spock raised his hand in the ancient Vulcan gesture of greeting and farewell. "Live long and prosper, Father."

When the screen faded away, Spock stared into the distance for a long time, not really seeing anything.

More weeks passed. Sarek returned home. He spoke to his son of the coming year when Spock would enter the Science Academy as a full-time student. Spock listened gravely, nodded, and kept his trouble to himself. After a morning spent reviewing the subtle language of the successful Marathan treaty, Sarek looked at Spock for a long time before saying, "You will make a fine diplomat one day, Spock. Study your science if you must, but realize that you have a higher calling. It is an infinitely varied galaxy, with much trouble in it. You can help to end hostility, to make the universe a more rational place as I have done."

Spock hoped that his face did not show the turmoil in his heart.

On a warm afternoon not long after, he found Amanda working in her garden. The sun was low, and the heat of the afternoon was pleasant in his bones. He helped his mother with an exotic Earth plant, and she spoke of it as they watered and pruned. "It's called a century plant," she said.

"Why is that?" asked Spock.

"There's a legend that it blooms only once every hundred Earth years." Amanda took a step back. "Well, it seems to be adapting nicely to Vulcan conditions."

"Does it?"

Amanda glanced at him. "Does it bloom only once a

century? No, actually it doesn't. It's more like once every twenty years or so."

"An illogical name," Spock observed.

Amanda laughed. "Well, we humans are an illogical species."

Spock looked around the garden. "This is a very harmonious place," he said. "You have planted species from forty-nine different worlds. It ought to be a jumble of competing forms and shapes, but it is not. There is a sense here of . . ." His voice trailed off. "Of completeness," he finished at last.

"Thank you, Spock."

"I am reminded of the *Enterprise*."

Amanda laughed again. "The connection escapes me."

On the horizon the sun sank. Soon the chill of night would come, the thin air releasing the heat of the day. Spock looked up. High in the darkening sky, wispy ice clouds caught the rays of the vanishing sun and glowed a brilliant scarlet. Beyond them was the darkness of space. Slowly, Spock said, "The *Enterprise* crew was not made up exclusively of humans. There were Centaurians, at least one Andorian, and a Betazoid as well. And one of the crew's parents were a Deltan and a human."

"Oh," Amanda said. "I see. They were many alien species all planted in one garden. Is that it?"

"Not planted, for they are all sentient," Spock said. "The Vulcan Science Academy, by contrast, is a garden filled with varalinths."

"Weeds?" Amanda shook her head. "Now you have lost me."

"A varalinth is not a weed," Spock said. "It is a Vulcan plant."

"I know, Spock," Amanda replied. "It branches roots far and wide, and wherever they approach the surface, they send up shoots that become clones identical to the parent plant. But to tell you the truth, varalinths are not particularly lovely specimens. They are adapted for harsh conditions, but they crowd out other plants."

"And so do the students at the Science Academy."

Amanda led him to the sheltered seat. "This is a more serious conversation than I thought," she said. "Tell me everything, Spock."

For the better part of an hour, Spock told her the whole story. He spoke of how he had felt like an outsider at the Science Academy but as if he belonged aboard the *Enterprise*. He told of Christopher Pike's surprising offer, of the fascination it held for him. To be the first Vulcan officer in Starfleet—that was an intriguing goal. "And it is logical," Spock said slowly. "Father has struggled to forge closer ties between Vulcan and the Federation. To have Vulcans in Starfleet can only help both Starfleet and ourselves."

"If you feel strongly about Starfleet," Amanda said, "you must accept the offer."

"Feelings are illogical, Mother."

"Not always, Spock."

With a sigh, Spock looked up. It was night now, and stars glittered overhead. "Father has planned my whole future for me," he said. "And he does not think highly of humans."

"With at least one exception, I hope."

Spock said, "I regret my—"

"Oh, hush, Spock. I'm joking."

"Yes." Spock sighed. "Father will not be pleased," he said at last.

After a long silence, Amanda said, "In an ancient Earth play, a character says, 'This above all: To thine own self be true.' He wasn't a very bright character, but that was a good piece of advice. And another work of literature from Earth, a poem, talks of choosing a path less traveled. It may create problems, but could you honestly take the path your father has made and not feel regret?"

"No," Spock said. "I would try to suppress the emotion, of course. But I would feel regret."

"When must you decide?"

"I have already decided," confessed Spock. "I will accept the appointment to Starfleet Academy. I must give my answer to Starfleet soon."

"I'll tell your father if you wish."

"No," Spock said. "That is my task." He looked up again. The stars, brilliant and fierce in the thin air of Vulcan, beckoned from the depths of space. "The motto of Starfleet Academy is also from an old Earth tongue," he said. *"Ex Astris, Scientia."*

"That's Latin," Amanda said. "From the stars, knowledge." In the darkness, she touched his arm. "But I know a better motto for you, Spock. *Ad Astra."*

"Yes," murmured Spock. "To the stars."

To the stars!

About the Authors

BRAD and BARBARA STRICKLAND are a husband-and-wife writing team who have co-authored three spooky books in the Are You Afraid of the Dark? series: *The Tale of the Secret Mirror, The Tale of the Phantom School Bus,* and *The Tale of the Deadly Diary.* They have also written two books about young Jean-Luc Picard in the Starfleet Academy series: *Starfall* and *Nova Command.* On his own, Brad did two Deep Space Nine books, *The Star Ghost* and *Stowaways.* Brad teaches English at Gainesville College, and Barbara is a second-grade teacher at Myers School. The Stricklands live in Oakwood, Georgia. They have a son, a daughter, and numerous pets, including two ferrets who always travel through the house at warp seven or faster.

About the Illustrator

TODD CAMERON HAMILTON is a self-taught artist who currently lives in Kalamazoo, Michigan. He has been a professional illustrator for the past ten years, specializing in fantasy, science fiction, and horror. Todd is the current president of the Association of Science Fiction and Fantasy Artists. His original works grace many private and corporate collections. He has co-authored two novels and several short stories. When he is not drawing, painting, or writing, his interests include metalsmithing, puppetry, and teaching.